And Alex Still Has Acne

Margaret Egrot

And Alex Still Has Acne

Cover Art:
Michelle Crocker

http://mlcdesigns4you.weebly.com/

Publisher's Note:

This is a work of fiction. All names, characters, places, and
events are the work of the author's imagination.

Any resemblance to real persons, places, or events is
coincidental.

Solstice Publishing - www.solsticepublishing.com

And Alex Still Has Acne
Margaret Egrot

Dedication:

In memory of my father – Ted Cowen.

Chapter One

The school bell rang to mark the end of the first lesson of the afternoon. Without showing a trace of sarcasm Miss Smith, the French teacher, thanked the class for being such an attentive bunch and, with a sigh of relief, gathered up her books and retreated for the staff room. A pity, she thought, that smoking was banned everywhere on school grounds – she could really do with a cigarette now. Year 10 was always hard work, especially first thing on a Friday afternoon.

Several students let out a whoop of delight as she left. In her rush to get out of the classroom, Old Smithers (she must have been at least 50) had forgotten to set them homework again. No doubt they would each get an email telling them to revise French verbs or something in time for the lesson on Monday, but they could always deny opening the email on the grounds they never switched on their computers at the weekend. As if!

Sam Rainsworth was slower than the others to collect his books and pens and stuff them into his school bag. He had hardly registered the start of the lesson, let alone the end. And Miss Smith, glad to have a quiet pupil not causing any trouble, had been happy to let him sit dreamily at the back of the class. He got up thoughtfully and left the classroom without speaking to anyone. At the corner of the corridor he found his friend, Alex, waiting for him.

"You OK? Thought you'd gone to sleep in Old Smithers' class just then." Alex loomed over him. A year ago both boys had been the same height, Sam just a little thicker set. But Alex had been going through a growing spurt and was now almost a head taller. He hadn't grown out sideways though and looked chronically under-nourished despite an enormous appetite. 'Legs like knotted string,' his mother often said about him, much to his embarrassment.

Sam looked up at his friend. "Yep, I'm fine. I was just thinking, that's all."

Sam carried on down the corridor instead of turning left towards the labs.

"Hey, where are you going?"

"Dunno, home I s'pect."

"It's not home time yet, we've got double physics, remember?"

Sam gave a mirthless smile. "It's an infringement of my human rights to have double physics last thing on a Friday. Besides I haven't done the homework."

"I have..."

"Smart-arse."

"No, I mean you can copy mine during the lesson and hand it in at the end – Parky never takes the books in till the end."

Sam paused for a moment, as if thinking about it. He leant down and pulled at one of his socks, then the other. Then he ran a hand through his hair, ruffling it up even more than usual. Finally he looked up at his friend and shook his head.

"Thanks, but no thanks. I'm not in the mood."

He turned from his friend and set off back down the corridor. He wasn't surprised though to hear lolloping footsteps behind him and to feel a hand on his shoulder. He knew who it was without turning round.

"So, you can resist the lure of physics too then?"

"I like physics, believe it or not," Alex said. "But you don't look right – I'm coming with you."

"Suit yourself."

Sam shrugged and continued walking in silence out of the school building, across the yard and down the short drive to the main road. Alex walked along beside him, hunched into his parka hood and whistling softly under his breath.

"I wish you'd cut that."

"Sorry?"

"That stupid whistling."

"Sorry, nervous tic. I was worried someone might spot us and haul us back."

"Well, you're safe now so you can shut up. You need more practice."

"Someone's going to catch up with you soon and write to your parents and then you'll be for it."

"As if they'll care ..."

"So your dad's really gone then? For good?"

"None of your business."

"Sorry, only my dad says ..."

"None of his business either."

"Sorry."

The pair walked on in silence for a couple of minutes. Then Sam felt inside his parka and drew out a couple of cigarettes and a lighter.

"Want one?"

"Where'd you get those from?"

"Mum. She's started smoking again since Dad's gone."

"Won't she notice two missing?"

"Nah. I took them from different packets earlier in the week. She couldn't tell. She's too pissed to notice much by bedtime these days."

"You mean she's drinking? I never thought your mum would do anything like that. She seems so..."

"Refined? Me neither. Never saw her drink anything more than a small glass of wine with a meal before. She's different now – sort of lost."

The boys continued for a while again in silence. Alex couldn't help noticing that his friend too had a lost look about him. But he had no idea what to do about it. Perhaps just sticking with him for the rest of the afternoon would be a start. After a few long minutes he said: "Well, what are we going to do? No point going into town – I'm skint."

"Me too, almost. Could we go over to your place?"

"Nah. Dad's home. He'd slaughter me if I came home from school too early. He's into school in a big way at the moment. Wants me to do well in GCSEs and so on and go to university. It'd be like his world had fallen in if he found out I'd bunked a lesson. What about your place?"

"Nah, not yet. Too empty when Mum's not there; too gloomy when she is. Later perhaps – let's go out on the town first. I've probably got enough for a burger and Coke at McDonald's."

"That's settled then. I'm starving."

"Why am I not surprised?" Alex's appetite was legendary.

They turned their feet in the direction of the golden arch, a new sense of purpose quickening their step. McDonald's was pretty full, plenty of people their own age, though their grammar school uniforms, badly concealed under their parkas, marked them out from the other customers. But, after chasing the last crumbs out from the burger wrappers and draining their cans, both boys felt better. Sam even smiled.

Alex belched as he finished his last drop of Coke.

"Oops, pardon – could do with another one of those," he waved his empty Coke tin in Sam's direction.

"Sorry, no can do," he put all his money on the counter between them and counted it. "Only got 60p to my name until I see Dad."

Suddenly his mobile rang – "Speak of the devil," he said to no-one in particular and answered the phone. "Hello Dad."

Alex leant back so as not to eavesdrop, and attentively brushed a mass of crumbs off his chest onto the floor. He watched as his friend grunted and nodded his head to the faint mumbling he could hear coming from the phone.

"Yeah, great," Sam said eventually, without any visible sign of enthusiasm. "See you same time and place on Sunday."

He switched off and turned back to his friend. Alex could see from Sam's face that he didn't want to discuss the call further. He straightened up in his seat as Sam concentrated on gathering up all their food wrappers and depositing them in the waste bin. He looked with mock horror at the ring of crumbs around Alex's seat.

"God Alex, you're a messy eater! Well what'll we do now?"

Alex shrugged. "Dunno. It's still too early to go home."

"You can come back to my place for tea if you like. It's not so bad really, and I'm still hungry."

"Me too. What you got to eat at home?"

"Nothing, unless Mum's stocked the fridge since breakfast this morning, which, I think not. We'll have to get something on the way home."

"But you haven't got any money."

"So?"

"So?"

"So, what?"

"Sam, you're not going to nick stuff are you?"

"All property is theft. Weren't you paying attention in history last week? At least that's what I think that Marx bloke said. I need to eat to live and if Mum is too drunk to shop, I've got to find other ways of feeding us."

"Does your dad know?"

"Of course not! Do you think I'm going to shop her to him? Or myself for that matter."

"I see. But surely he could do something about it, if he knew?"

"Mind your own business, will you? This is my problem and I'll sort it in my own time. Now, are you coming back to my place for more food or not?"

Alex sat silently for several minutes. He had never knowingly broken the law before, apart from cycling on the pavement - but then his mother preferred him to do that than run risks on the road. He didn't like the idea at all. But Sam was his friend, and he didn't like to abandon him either. Moreover, despite himself, he felt a tingling of excitement at what Sam was proposing. Anyway, he could never knowingly give up an opportunity for more food these days.

"Where?" Sam knew his friend was not enquiring where his house was, and felt a glow of pleasure that Alex was in on this with him. He too felt a tingle of excitement, plus a mixture of guilt and fear - but not enough of either to stop him.

"The One-Stop. It's big enough to have blind corners and small enough to not have any security."

"You've done this before." It was a statement rather than a question.

Sam nodded. "A couple of times. Tried Waitrose first 'cos that's where I knew from Mum shopping there – but security follows you round like you are a criminal or something, so I got out of there quick and tried the One-Stop. Easy-peasy there."

***

And it was. At least for Sam it was. Alex was amazed at how smoothly Sam sauntered into the shop. Alex felt hot and sweaty as soon as they got inside and started to take his parka off, knocking into the column of trolleys as he did so. Sam and the shop assistant turned to see what the noise was. He felt his face go bright red, which he knew was not a pretty sight against his ginger hair, and shrunk his neck down into his shirt collar as he pushed the trolleys back into a straight line.

"Idiot," hissed Sam. "Where are you going to put the stuff if you've taken your coat off?"

"Sorry," Alex whispered back, pulling his coat back over his shoulders, shrinking down further into his collar, and picking up a basket as nonchalantly as he could. He couldn't help feeling furtive as he looked around him, and he took a sharp intake of breath as his eye caught the poster by the baskets:

'NO   SHOPLIFTING   –   WE   ALWAYS PROSECUTE!'

He stopped in his tracks, the basket dangling loosely on his arm.

"Idiot," Sam hissed again, and made to take the basket off him. Then he re-considered.

"No. Keep the basket; I've got a better idea for you. Take this money ..." – Sam handed over the 60p left from the McDonald's bill – "... and go round the shop to see if you can buy anything with it, then meet me outside."

Alex nodded. He could see he was going to be a liability if he stuck with his friend. He was also relieved that he was no longer involved, so couldn't be prosecuted. That he was now acting as a decoy to distract the sole sales assistant's attention, so in effect aiding and abetting the commission of a crime, didn't occur to him.

They met up again just round the corner from the shop. Alex held out a packet of chewing gum and 2p. Sam opened his parka and revealed a packet of bacon, a twin pack of sausage rolls, two jelly trifles and a bag of satsumas. Alex gaped.

"How the heck did you manage all that?"

"Not too bad today. I just grabbed stuff out of the chilled section whilst the assistant was watching you didn't nick anything in the sweets section, and picked the fruit up by the door on the way out. She just assumed I was with you – even gave me a smile!"

"Well ..." Alex was speechless for a minute. "I still don't think it's right."

"No? Well you try going hungry for a couple of

days and see how it feels. I used to feel like you – still do most of the time – but things are a bit different now. Anyway I only nick what I need to eat; only this time I've nicked stuff for you too. So you're going to have to come home with me now."

Alex knew there was some faulty logic in this, but he was partly too impressed, partly too loyal, to say any more. He just followed his friend meekly down the road and back to his house.

***

Alex remembered Sam's house from previous visits as warm and hospitable, if rather too smart for comfort. There was often a smell of expensive coffee, and sometimes even the smell of freshly baked bread. There would be flowers on the hall table and it was always spotlessly clean and tidy; unlike his own house where usually there was a random scatter of books and papers in the living room; a pile of clothes at the bottom of the stairs waiting to be taken up if it was clean - or out to the laundry room if it was dirty; and unwashed crockery in the kitchen sink – waiting there to be stacked in the dishwasher once someone had got round to unloading the clean stuff. Alex usually felt he should have combed his hair before he went in through Sam's front door, and would become acutely conscious of the scruffy state of his footwear once inside.

But not today. The house felt cold; there were no flowers in the hall; there were no aromatic smells coming from the kitchen; and there was dust everywhere.

"Hello?" Sam called out as he opened the front door. "Mum? Are you in? I've brought Alex back for tea. Don't worry; I've bought us some stuff on the way home." There was an echoing silence.

"Looks like she's out," he said more quietly. "Just a sec, I'll check she's not in bed."

He disappeared and Alex had a bit of time to look around. The contrasting bleakness of what he saw compared with what he had always seen before made him shiver involuntarily. If this is what happened when your parents split up he hoped it would never happen with him. It couldn't, surely?

His mum and dad didn't always hit it off – Dad would yell at Mum if he fell over the dirty laundry – again, and Mum would have a go at Dad for not taking the bins out on the right day – again, and they would both shout at him if he got detention for forgetting his games kit or not handing in his homework on time, or dropping a plate when emptying the dishwasher. Mostly he associated home with laughter and warmth. Family meals were chaotic as both Mum and Dad often worked into the evening, but he looked forward to them. Apart from the food, which was nothing special but usually filling, mealtimes were where everybody voiced an opinion on any topic under the sun, including his younger sister, Nicky. She, at least until recently, always seemed to make a point of arguing with him on just about everything - despite his consistently better exam results throughout school, and superior wisdom gained through being a) male and b) nearly eighteen months older. Nobody in the Stevens family seemed to mind, as they laughed and shouted over each other to prove a point, that the sausages were burnt and the mashed potato lumpy, and the milk for their tea was still in the bottle as Mr. Stevens said that was more hygienic than a jug.

Very different from any meals he'd had with Sam, where Sam's mother always got out the best china and the silver teapot with matching milk jug. He was too terrified of breaking anything to enjoy the perfectly cooked steak, or whatever else was put in front of him. Sam's dad was more relaxed, but he was rarely there because he had some high powered job that took him abroad several times a month.

Now this, this – bleakness. If he was aware of the contrast in less than five minutes, how much worse must it be for Sam?

"No, she's not there. She must be out." Sam returned down the stairs and shrugged.

"Aren't you worried?"

"No, she's out loads these days, just wandering around mostly. Drinks somewhere too – at least she comes home a bit pissed sometimes. Don't worry Alex, she'll be back. I was scared the first time but now it's sort of normal. First time it happened I thought she'd gone and done herself in or something, but she came back OK – just cried a lot. I don't see her do so much of that now, thank God – the crying I mean.

"Anyway – enough of that. Let's get cracking. At least if we get the grill going it'll warm the kitchen up a bit before the central heating kicks in." With that he turned up the thermostat on the central heating, pulled the packets of food out of the pockets inside his parka, switched on the grill - and got to work on making their tea.

While Sam cooked Alex cleared the table, found a couple of clean knives and forks, and rinsed a couple of plates and put them to drain.

"What do you want me to do with this?" He held up a phone he'd found under papers on the table.

"What? Oh that's Mum's. She can never remember to take it with her. Never remembers to charge it up either. Bet the battery's flat again. Yep, thought so. See if you can find a charger and plug it in will you – might be some messages on it."

"You're not going to read your mum's messages are you? My mum would kill me if I did that. Dad too."

"Well things are different here now. Besides Mum's never worked out how to text or stuff so I have to do it for her. Only difference is she's not always around when I do it these days! Come on, this stuff's ready now - we'll check her messages later."

The boys ate in companionable silence. Alex had to admit – though not to Sam – that it all tasted OK. Sausage rolls and grilled bacon, liberally doused in tomato ketchup, were both filling and tasty. Ditto the trifle. He didn't really have much room left for a satsuma, but he tried juggling with a couple, then three, then four. The fourth fell to the floor and in his effort to keep the others up in the air he trod on it with a fart-like squelch. Both boys looked down at the mess and giggled.

"Oops, sorry. Good job your mum's not here," said Alex as he picked the main part of the fruit off his shoe and put it into the bin. "Here, have you got a cloth? I'll mop the rest up for you."

Sam passed him some kitchen paper and they cleaned up the floor, neither commenting on the relative cleanness of the area they had wiped compared with the rest of the floor.

"Sorry about that," Alex said again, putting the last of the kitchen paper in the overflowing waste bin. "Need a bit more practice – not quite ready to run away and join the circus."

He was about to say more, but his phone pinged and he pulled it out of his trouser pocket and scrutinised the screen.

"Oh heck – message from my mum, wondering where I am. S'pose that means she's home too and she and Dad have got their act together and made tea." He rubbed his stomach. "God I'm a bit full, but I s'pose I can manage a bit more."

"S'pose you can too. Honestly Alex, I don't know where you put it all."

"I don't either. Mum says I must have hollow legs; or worms. Well, I'd better be off, unless....?" He looked at his friend questioningly.

"No, I'm fine. Mum'll be in soon, I'm sure." He started to clear the table.

"Ever thought to check out where she goes?"

Sam stopped what he was doing and stared at his

friend, a look of surprise on his face.

"Not till you mentioned it, no. But you're right. It would be good to know; just to check she's OK, or something. Why, you offering to come and help? Like you did in the One-Stop?"

"Don't. I'm no good for that sort of thing – too ginger for one thing, and too clumsy. But I'll go with you Monday if you like. Straight after school. OK?"

"OK. Well, see you Monday."

Alex meanwhile was texting his mother – *@ Sam's, on way home*.

He nodded to his friend. "Well, I'd best be off. Call me if you need me. If not, see you Monday."

He was out through the door with a bang, and Sam turned his attention despondently to the remaining dirty plates and glasses on the kitchen table. He looked at the kitchen clock. Time was getting on – where was Mum?

Chapter Two

Sam's mum let herself into the house at 9.10pm. She looked tired and slightly dishevelled. Her expensive beige Burberry trench coat was crumpled, as if she had hung it on the floor somewhere and put it on carelessly to come home. Her blonde hair, that always used to be so immaculate, was showing a mix of dark and grey at the roots and looked in need of a good comb through. Her knee length boots, bought some years ago at Harrods on one of her regular shopping trips to London, were scuffed and down at heel. She looked fragile and tearful as she crept into the living room where Sam was watching TV.

Sam, who was starting to feel that he was the parent these days, pressed the mute button on the remote and got up to help her off with her coat. Close up he could smell the drink on her. He could tell it wasn't whisky or beer – sherry? He wasn't sure – but she seemed steady enough on her feet. She pushed him away feebly and he sat back down.

"Been somewhere nice?"

"Oh, out and about you know..."

He resisted the urge to probe further, remembering how much he hated his parents quizzing him – back in the good old days, three or four months ago, when he had two parents at home who worried about such things. How he longed now for more of that unwelcome parental nosiness. How he wished he had appreciated it more at the time – perhaps then none of this would have happened. But no! He stopped himself following that line of self-doubt - he was sensible enough to know that his irritation about their interest and concern for him was pretty normal for parents and their teenage offspring – and nothing whatsoever to do with whatever else had gone wrong for them.

Instead he waited as she fumbled with her buttons, and then dropped her coat onto the arm of the sofa.

"Hungry?"

"No. I had something out. What about you? Was there anything...?" Her voice petered out as she sat herself carefully on the sofa next to Sam, and her eyes started to close.

"There's nothing in the fridge Mum. I got something in town and ate it with Alex. Mum!" He gave her a shake to keep her awake. "Mum!" He said again more loudly, "We've got to get some shopping in – we've run out of just about everything."

"But I haven't got any money."

"Yes you have. Dad still puts money into the account. And he'll give you cash if you ask for it. Yes he will! I know it. Look..." He got up and collected her mobile from the kitchen.

"See, I've opened your messages – the first is from Dad asking if you are OK and do you want anything – like more money. He says that so you shouldn't be afraid to ask. The second is from the library to say your books are overdue, and the third is from the hairdresser to find out why you missed your appointment today. Mum – oh Mum PLEASE try to keep awake – this is important!"

"Not now dear, please – we'll talk about it in the morning." His mother struggled to her feet. "I'm so tired; I think I'll just go to bed. We'll talk about it in the morning." She repeated.

"Like last weekend. Not." Sam mouthed after her and slumped back onto the sofa. Anyway, by the time she got up tomorrow he would be back at school for a rugby match. He had fought hard for his place in the under 15 1st team and he wasn't going to give it up lightly.

Should he tell his dad? Surely he would be worried too if he knew what was happening at home. But in that case why wasn't he at home? Sam had still not worked out why his dad had left three months ago. His parents never really rowed – unlike Alex's noisy and messy house where everyone carried on at top voice, his home if anything was always too quiet, and his parents didn't seem to have much to say to each other.

He had had no idea that they were unhappy – and neither would tell him straight just why his dad had left and was now in a flat in the next town – on his own as far as Sam could tell. It was a mystery to him. One thing he was sure of was that he had no part in the cause of the break up. But with Dad all tight lipped when they went out together on a Sunday, and his mum all weepy for the rest of the week, it seemed like he was going to have to play a part in sorting it out. Alex was right - and first of all they might as well find out what his mum got up to during the day, and where.

But before any of that he had to get his rugby kit together. It was a home game tomorrow, so he didn't have to be at the school till 9.30am for a 10 o'clock start, but all the same he didn't want to rush about in the morning – and he didn't want to run the risk of being late and being dropped from the team. Rugby on a Saturday was, at the moment, one of the few anchors for him in what - he found himself sniffing slightly - was turning out to be a pretty ghastly year.

He pulled himself together and heaved himself off the sofa, picking up his mother's coat as he did so. It was heavier than he expected and, after a moment's hesitation – but why not? After all he checked her mobile without feeling he was prying. He felt inside her pockets and pulled out several large stones and a note. He read the note and put the stones down on the side table by the sofa. What on earth did all this mean? Why would his mother, who always used to take a pride in looking smart, spoil the line of her coat by stuffing the pockets like this? And as for the note... He shook his head. None of it made sense, not at that time of night anyway.

Rummaging around in the kitchen, the downstairs

cloakroom and his bedroom he found all his rugby kit. It was still dirty from the last game. He picked away the mud from around the studs on his boots, and brushed and shook the loose mud from his shorts and top. Mr. Parks would make some sarcastic comment or other, but at least he had everything he needed, so tough. He was less cool though when he remembered his missed physics lesson. It would be a miracle if Parky had not noticed he was absent. Too late now – he would think of some excuse by the morning – maybe say his mother was ill and needed him at home or something on Friday afternoon – it was almost the truth.

That reminded him – where was she going these afternoons? And why stones in her pocket? Why that peculiar note? He certainly needed to check this out, and he was glad Alex had suggested trying to track her down. Not that Alex was any use for surveillance. He was too lanky, nobody could miss his red hair, and he was bound to bump into something, or drop it, or fall into it. But he was clever – he could be relied upon to come up with a good idea when needed. Most important of all he was his best friend, just as their dads had been best friends before them. Despite their many different interests Alex, he knew, could be relied upon whatever the situation. He'd do the same for his friend of course, but at the moment he was the one with the problem.

With luck, by the end of Monday evening, they would have a better understanding of what the problem was, and a better idea of what to do next.

Chapter Three

Nicky sat on the edge of her bed that Friday night. What had that last row with Alex been about? She didn't care a toss about his friend Sam – he of the golden tousled locks, the muscular legs, and the hand and foot co-ordination that got him into the first team for both cricket and rugby. He probably had loads of girlfriends anyway.

So why, when Alex rushed home late and said he'd spent the early evening with Sam, had she asked loudly at the table whether the pair of them were gay, or something? Alex had kicked her under the table, she had screamed, and Mum had tried to remonstrate both with Alex for using violence to sort an argument and with Nicky for being homophobic. She hadn't used that word of course, but Nicky knew what she meant. And, no, she wasn't at all against gays. She didn't care a bit about Sam and his friendship with her brother. And anyway she was sure he wasn't gay.

All the same, it would be nice if Sam noticed her a bit. She wasn't a kid anymore. Her thirteenth birthday had been months ago, and she had started wearing mascara – even for school – so she looked a lot older.

Perhaps she was too fat? She got up and looked in the mirror. A small, slight, dark-haired girl stared back at her. She didn't look at all like the rest of the family. Alex all gangly and clumsy like his dad, and red-headed like his mother. 'The Irish side coming out,' was what Mrs. Stevens used to say, proudly. No, she was just short and dark and squat – and everybody could see straight away that she must be adopted.

Not that that had bothered her at all until recently. She had loved her mum and dad without question from the moment she first met them when she was three years old, and moved to live with them permanently six months later.

She knew that they treated her exactly as they treated Alex – the same amount of telling off, the same amount spent on birthday and Christmas presents, the same number of hugs...

But recently she had felt there was something different between her and the rest of them. It was nothing to do with hair and skin colour, or even size – Alex had always been tall and skinny; she had always been the shortest in her class. No, recently she had realised something much more fundamental. They were all clever – seriously clever. She was just normal, average, middle of the road. And fat.

Now, when she joined in an argument, she felt they were just humouring her if they listened, and were careful not to put her down, though Alex sometimes forgot and called her a stupid cow – like he had just now over her comment about Sam before he kicked her. Maybe his verbal scorn was better – she could just shout back at him. Certainly better than Mum's careful and considered explanations as to why she may be wrong, or Dad's toe curling attempts to 'see things from her point of view'. Sometimes they were so reasonable she could scream.

She leant into the mirror, to examine the two additional tiny spots that had developed on her face since the morning. She had seven in all now. 'Acne,' she supposed grimly. 'At this rate I'll be covered by Monday.' At least she wasn't as spotty as Alex – he had quite a crop across his nose and even on his neck, and they showed up much worse on his pale skin. But there was no denying she was getting more like him on the bad skin front. This was one physical characteristic they had in common anyway, not that it was much comfort to her.

She stopped examining her face and turned to scrutinise the rest of her body in the mirror. She pulled at her clothes and posed from both sides. Way too short – such stumpy legs. And way, way too fat. Her mother wouldn't hear of it – size eight was NOT fat, she assured her, even for someone under 5ft 4in, but Nicky wasn't convinced. She had to get under size six. She looked gross at this size. She did not under any circumstances want to end up as fat as her mother, who must be a size 14 at least, and had started to wear those ghastly elastic-waisted skirts and trousers she said were more comfortable for a woman of her age. Nicky thought she'd never be seen dead in clothes like that, whatever her age.

She was glad now they had had that row at the table before the meal had started – she had been able to run up to her room and leave her food uneaten. At least she hadn't had to put up with her mother's gentle encouragement to eat a bit more, or she wouldn't grow any more. Didn't she understand? That was the whole point – she wouldn't mind being taller, but she didn't want to put on any more weight, not even a gram!

Tired at last of examining herself in the mirror, she picked up her phone. Three messages had arrived since she had last looked – two from friends asking if she had done her homework yet and, if so, what was the answer to the fourth question on the maths worksheet. The answer to both was 'no', but she could always get Alex to help her with the maths problem – if they were speaking again that evening that is.

The third text was more puzzling – it said simply *Why are you so fat?* Mirroring uncannily exactly the thoughts she had had about herself just now as she looked into the mirror. She looked round hastily – as if someone was in the room behind her, reading her mind. It was the third text she'd had like that. Not quite the same – the first had said *Why are you so ugly?* The second simply *Hi spotty!* Who was sending them? Not a friend surely? But who else knew her phone number?

She sat down on the bed, staring wet eyed at the small screen. She refused to let a little thing like this upset her. It was not going to make her cry – but the effort of stopping herself made her shake. 'But that's what I am,' she thought – 'a fat, ugly, spotty waste of space. They can't want me here – I don't look like any of them, and if I tell Mum about these she'll ask loads and loads of questions and then tell me not to let it bother me, which it doesn't anyway. Then she'd go and see the head teacher or something, and I'd die of embarrassment. I might tell Alex, except I'm not speaking to him ever again. Anyway he might just laugh and say he agrees with them. If only I had a proper mother. Maybe I do – it's just a matter of looking.'

She gave a big sniff, shuffled along her bed to the little desk at the foot, and switched on her laptop that her parents had given her for her 13th birthday. It was neat and light, with a pink cover, and Alex had linked it up to the internet for her. She was very proud of it, even taking it into school recently to complete a special project. She switched it on and typed in her password. She knew she should start her homework first, but a quick online chat wouldn't do any harm surely? She logged into her Facebook page and reeled back in horror – someone had replaced her photo with a close up of a pig in a tutu standing on its hind legs. This time she screamed out loud.

Alex, who was passing her room on the way to his, paused outside her door. He was still annoyed at what she had said about his friend, and cross with his mother for telling him off, but she did sound upset. He knocked her door briefly and went straight in without waiting for permission.

"What's up, Sis?"

She pointed mutely at the screen. Alex's first impulse was to laugh – the pig photo was very funny – but he squashed this impulse quickly as he could see she was upset.

"Who did that? Not you presumably?"

She shook her head. "I don't know. It wasn't there

this morning."

"Want me to put your proper one back?" Alex didn't wait for her to reply, just took the laptop and fiddled around until her original photo was back in place – it was he who had set up her link in the first place.

"There you go." For the first time since he had entered the room he looked properly at his sister and noticed the tearful look.

"Hey Sis, what's up? Not still mad at me surely? If so, I'm sorry – I was out of order."

"Me too. I shouldn't have said that about you and Sam. No, it's this." She showed him the texts.

He whistled softly.

"Hey, there's someone out there doesn't seem to like you much. You should tell Mum."

"No! She'd make a big thing of it. I'll just delete them. There!"

Alex put his hand out, but was too late to stop her.

"People shouldn't send things like that – they're only words, but they're upsetting. Don't delete them. You've got to tell someone, even if it's only me. But it'd be better to tell Mum or Dad."

"No! Mum'd make such a meal of it. Besides, she's not my proper mum."

Alex was shocked.

"Don't say that! Course she is. As good as anyway. What did your real mum do for you except put you in care when you were a baby?"

"We don't know that do we? That's just the story I've been told. There might have been a good reason why she couldn't look after me at the time. Things might be different now. She might be out there looking for me right now."

"Well she'd have a bit of a problem – there must be thousands of girls of your age called Nicky, and hundreds with the surname Stevens. It's not like you'll be listed

25

under your old name anywhere. Now 'Hitchin' – that would have been easy enough to track down – especially as it's with an 'i' not an 'e'. Anyway, Mum said she'd help you find her with a social worker when you're a bit older, but you've always said you didn't want to."

"Maybe I've changed my mind."

Alex looked at her. "Maybe you have. Well it's your life. I probably would too if I were you. Are you OK now as I s'pose I'd better go and do my homework?"

"Me too. Yes I'm fine. Well, sort of. Thanks Alex."

"No probs. Any time." He got up from the little chair by the desk, punched his sister playfully on the shoulder – though it still hurt enough to make her wince - and left the room.

"Yes, thank you very much, Alex," she said silently to the closing door. "You've given me a great idea." By the time the door was properly shut she was back on the computer feverishly tapping 'Hitchin' into Google.

Chapter Four

Monday dragged for Sam. He only just made it into school before the first lesson of the morning so did not have time to chat with Alex about the weekend. They met up during the break, but as he had not done his history homework, he spent the time huddled in a corner of the library with Alex's homework in front of him – copying it all down with a few strategic alterations and some spelling mistakes. Alex sat beside him, whistling softly under his breath. It was as irritating to Sam as it always had been, but he realised it would be ungrateful to tell him to shut up whilst copying his homework, so he bit his tongue and carried on writing at speed.

"There," he said at last. "Never knew I was so clever – where did you find out all that stuff anyway?"

"Mum," Alex replied. "She's got a degree in history – joint honours in fact, in history and English literature. It's shutting her up once she gets going that's the problem. Oh damn! There's the bell. And it's PE – God how I hate PE! I wish I'd got a sprained ankle or something."

Still grumbling, he put his homework back in his bag and waited for his friend to pack his stuff away too.

Sam was pleased though. He found it hard to concentrate in the classroom these days, but doing something physical still appealed to him. It helped him take his mind off his parents and their separate miseries. He'd had a good enough time with his dad on Sunday; they had been to watch his dad's old team play rugby, and then gone for a meal, where his dad had shown just about enough interest in Sam's game for the school on Saturday, and his winning try. Sam could see that his dad's heart wasn't in it really though. He could see that he was making an effort, and appreciated it. But when he was not actually asking or answering questions, his dad's attention drifted - as did his own. So there were a lot of long periods of silence during their day out.

At one point his dad asked: "Did your mum get my message?" Sam nodded, and tried to find words to express his concerns about her, but none came to him so he kept quiet. His dad also looked as if he wanted to say more, but was struggling to find suitable words. Sam could understand this. How do you ask your 14-year-old son about your wife – his mum – without making the situation worse? So both retreated into silence for much of the time they were together. It had been a good enough day; but it could have been so much more, and Sam worried that neither his mum nor dad were any happier for being apart. What would make them happier? Was it his job to make them happy? What about him in all this? His own life was hardly a barrel of laughs at the moment.

It was thoughts like these that Sam wanted to avoid. French, history, maths, etc. didn't provide enough of a distraction. But PE was different. Unlike Alex, who was often the butt of other boys' jokes, having at least three left feet, Sam was naturally sporty and could run faster than most boys his age, tackle harder in rugby, and catch 'impossible' balls in cricket. So he headed towards the gym with a feeling almost approaching enthusiasm. It was not until lunchtime that he and Alex talked about the plan to track down his mother after school.

"You still on for this?" he asked, as they munched their sandwiches in the canteen.

"Sure," Alex replied. "Do you have any ideas where to start?"

"Nope, but here's something you can think about during the rest of the day. When I went to hang my mother's coat up after she came in on Friday night, I checked her pockets – no don't look at me like that – I'm worried about her, remember? Anyway, whatever you think about it, I had a rummage in her coat pockets and found a couple of odd things alongside the old paper tissues and stuff that you'd expect."

"What?" Alex was interested now.

"A pile of old stones – about the size of hockey balls, but marbled and really heavy – and a note. It wasn't an odd note in itself – it was just a reminder from the library that the books she'd had from the library were overdue. What's odd is Mum never reads proper books and this note was over a week old. It was for books by someone called Virginia Woolf or something!"

"Oh her! My mum is always raving about her."

"Yes, but that is your mum. My mum isn't like that; I didn't even know she had joined the library – Dad and I haven't – and Virginia Woolf? I wouldn't have even heard of her myself if I hadn't seen her books round at your house, and your mum had told us a bit about her. Surely nobody ever reads her these days – apart from your mum of course; but she's a bit weird like that!"

"Charming! I'm not sure where any of that will lead us and I really think I've got a headache coming on. I'm going to see if I can skip PE."

"You coward you – they'll never believe you, and you'll end up with detention instead! But thanks for your support and, if I miss you in lessons, I'll meet you by the school gates around 3.30."

***

Shortly after 3.30 the boys met up again, Alex's headache miraculously gone, and Sam feeling much better following a good workout in the gym – subsequent lessons had gone quite smoothly after that – he'd almost concentrated like normal. The fact that he and Alex had a plan to work on later that day made him feel almost optimistic again.

"Right, where do we start?" Alex smoothed down his dishevelled ginger locks that were blowing about in the autumn wind, whipped out a magnifying glass that he had kept for this moment and put it to his eye. He clowned about trying to look sharp and sleuth-like. Sam laughed.

"Put that thing away you idiot! This is serious. I'll ring home and check Mum's not there first. This search may well turn out to be a wild goose chase, but at least we can check whether the goose is at large or not." He pressed the keys on his phone as he spoke and both boys heard the phone ring out repeatedly.

"Nope. She's not there. And the answerphone's not on so she's had plenty of time to pick up if she was there. So – game on!"

"Where do we start?" Alex had put his magnifying glass away by this time, and was looking enquiringly at his friend.

Sam shrugged. "Not sure, seems disloyal somehow, spying on her and all that. Perhaps it wasn't such a good idea after all."

"And doing nothing is an even worse idea. Come on, you can't back out now you've got me in tow. You say she's been coming home drunk?" Alex saw his friend wince. "Well you think she may've had a drink or two before she gets back home then?"

Sam nodded.

"Right, let's wander into town and pop our heads into all the wine bars that look like a respectable looking woman like your mum might feel she could go into alone."

"They'll never let us in, we're much too young, and if we did get in and she saw us well, it would be just too embarrassing...."

"Well we just say we're looking for our older brother, or dad or something, have a quick glance from the door and then leg it; no need for her to see us at all, let alone speak to us."

Sam shrugged again. "OK, let's go."

Chapter Five

S am and Alex thought they must have been into every wine bar and pub in town that was open between 3.30pm and 6pm. Most of the early ones they went into were almost deserted, some of the later ones had started to fill with office workers stopping off for a drink or two before facing the commute back home – or whatever it was back home that they needed a drink to face, Sam had commented wryly. But his mother wasn't in any of them and the two boys began to feel it was a pointless task, and they might as well go home. Alex, for one, was starving, and Sam too had to admit to feeling a bit peckish.

"I've got some cold pizza left over from a takeaway Dad bought just before I came home last night. It's probably a bit dry by now, but you're welcome to share it if you want."

"It's food isn't it?" said Alex, perking up a bit at the prospect of anything basically edible. "What're we waiting for?"

The boys let themselves into Sam's house and Sam called out to see if his mum was home. There was no reply, and a quick check of all the rooms confirmed for him that she was definitely out. While he was upstairs Alex had found the pizza and, as he had learnt from his mum (an expert in resuscitating dubious oddments in the fridge), he sprinkled it with water, added a bit of tomato ketchup and put it in the microwave for two minutes. By the time Sam returned there was an almost appetising smell filling the kitchen and the boys ate ravenously.

"Well, what now?" asked Alex after a while, as he wiped cheesy smears off his shirt with the inside of his blazer.

"There's no more food I'm afraid."

"No, stupid, I meant what now about tracking down your mum."

"Oh. I'm not so sure it's a good idea after all."

Alex looked at his friend exasperatedly.

"You can't pack in now – we've hardly started. And shouldn't you be more worried that she wasn't in any of the places you expected, rather than less?"

"Course I'm worried – just don't know what to do for the best."

"Well," said Alex, looking meaningfully at the mobile phone tucked into the corner of the table. "You could check her messages again."

Sam raised his eyebrows. "You've changed your tune."

Nonetheless he reached across and picked up the phone, grimacing at the screen as he punched various keys.

"Nope, nothing new – apart from another message from the library, which I think she must have listened to as it's listed as saved. She has got as far as putting the books together on the sideboard see – just gone out and forgotten to take them with her I s'pose."

"Maybe," Alex fidgeted on his seat and there was a silence between the boys for a few minutes, broken only by Alex's soft whistling under his breath. Sam was just about to burst out with an irritated 'Jesus Alex! Stop that blasted noise,' when Alex stopped of his own accord and looked at his friend.

"Well, we haven't achieved much today, and I've got to get back for tea and to do my homework, but I can take the books back to the library on my way – maybe a visit there will provide me with a bit of inspiration."

Sam didn't comment on Alex's capacity for a second tea, but he liked the idea of the library.

"I'll come too – there's bound to be a fine to pay, and I've still got money from Dad. Here, help me put this stuff in the dishwasher first."

It didn't take them long to reach the library, and Alex wasn't that surprised to meet his mother on her way out; an avid reader, she always had several books on the go. She, however, was surprised to see them.

"Hello boys! Whatever next – what brings you here?"

"Oh, hello Mrs. Stevens. We're just bringing Mum's books back as they're overdue."

"Ah yes – Virginia Woolf. Did she like them? I bumped into her a couple of months ago and we came in here for a coffee. I told her you're never alone if you have a good book to read. I'm not sure she believed me, but she joined up anyway. I'm not sure either that Woolf was the best choice for her, but she was rather taken with the idea. It's worried me since, because I think she was mainly interested in her because I said she was someone who always tried to be upbeat despite recurring mental health problems. But then she took her own life anyway, when she felt she couldn't cope with another bad spell, so perhaps she wasn't the best example I could have picked. Jane Austen for instance, she ..."

Sam, who hadn't been paying much regard to Mrs. Stevens up till then – he knew from of old that she loved to bring a little English or history lesson into all her conversations, especially with young people – turned his full attention on her.

"This Woolf woman committed suicide?"

"Yes indeed, so sad, she filled her pockets with stones and walked into the river and drowned herself."

Sam dumped the books on the counter without listening any more to either Mrs. Stevens or the librarian who was demanding £2.50 in fine money.

"Oh God," he said as if to himself. "That explains it – I've got to go."

He rushed off. Alex looked at his mum who was staring after him in astonishment. Alex made to dash after him but Mrs. Stevens caught his arm.

"What's happening? What's the matter with Sam?

Is he all right?" she asked urgently as Alex tried to pull away from her.

"Not really, he's been worried about his mum's odd behaviour recently – and why she had stones in her coat pocket. Now he thinks he knows, thanks to you," her son replied. "Anyway, I'm going after him. Save some tea for me."

Then he too rushed off, ignoring his mother's call to make sure he was back in time to do his homework or his dad would be after him. Alex's behaviour recently was puzzling her; maybe Sam wasn't being a very good influence on him at the moment – one of their neighbours had reported seeing both boys in town last week during school hours, and she would need to talk to him about this when he sat still for five minutes. She was also worried – had her good intention of trying to get her son's best friend's mother to take an interest in reading to distract her from her problems gone badly wrong? She was sure Sam's mother was OK. 'Only a boy's overactive imagination would put two and two together and make five,' she told herself. Anyway, she would ring Sam's house later tonight and, she was sure, speak directly to his mother, who would be bound to have a straightforward explanation.

There was no denying it was a bit odd though, she thought, as she offered a £5 note at the counter for Mrs. Rainsworth's and her own overdue books and received £1.50 in change. But, she told herself firmly, there was nothing she could do just standing in the door of the library 'worriting', as she called it. She was much better going back home and putting some supper together. Alex was bound to be home soon, possibly with Sam in tow; her husband would be back from the university and probably starving as he never seemed to stop for lunch and there was Nicky to think of too.

Ah yes, Nicky. Nicky had changed recently; the noisy, cheerful, opinionated little girl they had adopted when she was only three had been replaced by a moody, angry, teenager. Now, instead of taking over the conversation at meal times, and seizing control of the remote whenever she got the chance, she preferred to spend time on her own in her room and was, Mrs. Stevens was very much afraid, developing 'food issues' - not something she or the male members of the family had ever suffered from, so she wasn't sure quite how to handle it. In fact, she thought almost crossly, she had enough of her own family problems to worry about without taking on Sam's family problems too.

She gathered up her new books, almost forgetting to thank the librarian on her way out, and stomped home - her normally sunny nature unusually subdued.

Chapter Six

Alex caught up with Sam at the end of the road.
"There's probably no connection at all you know. Between your mum and that writer, I mean."

"Sure," Sam grunted, but he didn't slacken his pace.

"So, where are you going?"

"Home, I need to check something."

"Stones?"

Sam nodded. "I can't remember if they were at home or not when we had tea. I must check first."

Alex was relieved, he didn't fancy tearing round town again on the off chance of tracking down Sam's mother – he had homework to do, and was starting to feel peckish again. He was sure also that he had seen the stones on the side table at Sam's house. He settled his stride to fit with Sam's.

"OK, I'll come with you."

Sam didn't speak, but nodded and touched his friend's arm as if to acknowledge him and say thank you. The two carried on together, walking briskly and determinedly towards Sam's house.

The lights were on in the hall at Sam's house when they arrived. Alex didn't think that either he or Sam had switched them on when they went out, and hoped that this meant that Mrs. Rainsworth was back home. Sam too looked optimistic and quickened his pace even more, so that the two boys were almost running when they reached the front door. It was locked as usual, and Sam searched for his key while Alex whistled softly under his breath.

"Where the hell did I put it? Ah here, thank God." Sam retrieved his key, put it into the lock and opened the door.

"Mum?" he called out hopefully as he entered the hall. There was no reply, and both boys could see now that there were no other lights on in the house. Also the heating had not yet been switched on, and the air struck them as almost as chilly as the external autumn air.

"Damn," said Sam softly, "I was hoping..."

"Me too."

A noise from the front room distracted them and both boys tiptoed across the hall, Sam first and Alex close behind. Despite the gathering dusk, he could see over Sam's shoulder that there was something on the sofa. It was the recumbent body of a woman, with faded blonde hair dressed in a beige raincoat. She was snoring softly, with an occasional louder rattle in the back of her nose – the noise that had alerted the boys initially to her presence. It had to be Sam's mum, and Alex was glad for Sam's sake that she was obviously home and safe. But Alex was not a complete idiot either. He could smell the alcohol from the doorway and this was no ordinary nap.

No. Mrs. Rainsworth was definitely and decisively drunk and unconscious to the world. Alex felt embarrassed for Sam that his mum should be seen like this – she who had always been so cool and elegant on his previous visits. He turned away and took himself off into the kitchen, but not before noticing with relief that the stones were on the side table where he thought he had last seen them. At least she had not taken them out with her; and her coat and hair – as best as he could see – had been bone dry as she lay sleeping on the sofa.

He sat down at the table and wondered what was best to do next. He should get home – but he couldn't just leave the house without talking to Sam first. In the background he could hear his friend trying to rouse his mother, but he knew this was a thankless task. Only a few weeks ago Nicky had come home from an evening out blind drunk and fallen asleep on the sitting room floor.

His parents had been shocked and tried to rouse her – mostly, he realised afterwards, to check she had not taken drugs. But no, she had simply been in with the wrong crowd who had spent several hours after school mixing Red Bull and vodka. Nicky, as the newcomer to the group, had been forced into some kind of initiation rite and had drunk far too much. Not being used to alcohol in anything like that quantity and being slight of frame, she rapidly succumbed and it was a wonder she had actually got home on her own that evening. Eventually their mum simply brought her duvet down from her bed and put it over her to keep her warm, and placed a basin by her head in case she was sick.

When his dad returned home he carried her up to bed and it was then that they all found out that she had wet herself. There was still the faint outline on the sitting room carpet, despite his mum's best efforts to remove it. He shuddered slightly – so this is what Sam will have to face with his mum in the morning. 'Would this be for the first time?' he wondered.

A few minutes later, Sam came out into the kitchen. He flicked the central heating thermostat up till the boiler kicked in and sat down heavily at the kitchen table, his head in his hands. After a couple of minutes he looked up.

"Alex, I've never seen her like this before. I don't know what to do."

Alex thought back to what he had witnessed at home a few weeks ago.

"You sure it's just drink?"

"Pretty sure – she must've bought some sherry while she was out. There's a large bottle by the sofa and it's nearly all gone. I'm sure she isn't used to drinking in that sort of quantity, and she's not eating properly."

"Well," said Alex, "I know a bit about this sort of thing." He wasn't going to tell on Nicky despite Sam's enquiring look.

"What you need to do..." he went on, "...is to just let her sleep it off. I'd bring her duvet or a blanket down to keep her warm, and a pillow for her head. Maybe a bowl in case she's sick. She should be fine in the morning, apart from a hangover. Oh and…' he paused, not sure how to put this delicately, "Sam, you may find she's wet herself when she wakes up."

"Oh, God, not Mum!" Sam looked horrified.

Alex took a brisk line – he was too embarrassed himself to try to be diplomatic.

"Look, it could be a lot worse. She's here and she's basically safe. And the stones – they were where you left them last night. Whatever she's got them for; it's not what you're worried about. She'll be OK when she wakes up, but you must tell your dad she needs some help – or get her to see a doctor or something. She can't go on like this – and you can't either."

Sam shook his head. "I can't think straight right now. I'll think about it in the morning. Maybe I'd better skip school to see she's OK. I'll try talking to her too. Meanwhile I'll chuck the rest of this sherry down the sink – unless you want some?" he added with a feeble attempt at humour.

"Hell no! Not my favourite tipple at all." Alex also tried not to be too heavy.

"Nor mine." Sam picked up the bottle, uncorked it and tipped the remaining couple of inches down the sink. He then rinsed the bottle and went to put it into the bulging recycling bin. As he moved the papers on top to find room for the bottle he uncovered three other large – and empty – sherry bottles. So tonight's drinking was not a one off! From the intake of breath and low whistle behind him he realised that Alex had seen the bottles too.

He swirled round to look straight at his friend, a strange look of hostility in his eyes.

"Don't you dare tell anybody!"

Alex made to protest. "But my mum; she knows what to do in these situations, she…"

"Especially not her! Mum sees her as a friend – she

doesn't seem to have many others. She'd feel so ashamed if your mum found out. You mustn't tell anyone, do you hear? If you do I'll never speak to you again."

Chapter Seven

After Alex had gone, looking a little hurt at the harsh way his friend had spoken to him, Sam stared at the empty sherry bottle still in his hand and sighed. He almost wished he hadn't emptied it out – he could do with something to cheer himself up. Not that the sherry would have been particularly good at that – there wasn't enough of it left, for one thing, and he rather disliked the taste – associating it with Christmas and New Year and old people like his grandmas and aunties taking 'just a little drop' to show they were all good sorts willing to join in with the festive spirit. He didn't really associate it with people like his mum – so why was she now obviously drinking it in considerable quantity?

Quickly, he stuffed the bottle alongside the others as far down the bin as it would go and went back into the front room to check on her. She was still sleeping as he'd left her. Gently he shook her by the shoulder. Then again, a little less gently. But she shrugged him away without opening her eyes and settled her head more deeply into the sofa cushions. He sighed again and, remembering what Alex had advised - how did he know all this, he wondered - he went upstairs to fetch his mother's duvet and a bowl. He wrapped the duvet round her loosely and placed the bowl on the floor at her side. Then, sighing yet again, he dimmed the lights in the room, closed the door and went back into the kitchen. Somehow or other he needed to get his homework done. Even if he didn't go into school tomorrow morning, it was better to get it out of the way.

An hour and two cups of tea later, he had finished all the homework he intended to do that night. It wasn't his best effort – he needed Alex or his dad on hand to achieve that – but it was, he felt, a good enough effort to keep the teachers off his back and stop them asking awkward questions.

He was dog tired. He looked at his watch. Still only 9.30pm, but it felt like the middle of the night. He got up and went into the front room to look again at his mother. She was sleeping just as he'd left her. Clearly she was not going to wake up this side of midnight, so there was no point staying up to talk to her. They would have to have a chat tomorrow. But what about exactly? He tried a few opening gambits:

"Hi Mum, are you turning into an alcoholic?"

"Mum, I've been doing a bit of shoplifting recently; on account of you never getting me any food."

"Mum, are you ill?"

"Why have you and Dad split up?"

"Don't either of you care about me anymore?"

None of these questions seemed right, though they were all ones he wanted answers to, especially the last, although he was a bit ashamed to admit this – even to himself. He was fourteen going on fifteen after all. He was sorry now he had been so harsh with Alex. He was his best friend, almost his only friend outside the sports teams at the moment, and he genuinely wanted to help. But Sam felt that already he had let him into far more of his family's problems than was right. After all, Alex hadn't confided anything like that to him – but maybe that was because his own home life was so trouble free. So how could he properly understand what he, Sam, was going through? All the same, Sam realised, he shouldn't have snapped at his friend like that. He suddenly felt very alone, without anyone to chat to before settling in for the night.

He took out his phone, and before setting off upstairs to bed sent his friend a quick text. *Sorry. Out of order. Spk soon. Thanks. Sam.* He was a bit surprised not to get a text straight back – it was unlike Alex. Perhaps he really had upset him this time. Well he couldn't worry about that now. He was shattered and could scarcely summon the energy to clean his teeth and wash his face before falling into bed – where he slept right through to his alarm at 7.45am the next day.

Alex had read the text all right. But he had too much else on his mind to reply straight away. He understood why his friend had bitten his head off – he'd have done the same if he had been in Sam's place - if he hadn't died of embarrassment first. He could just imagine his own feelings if he and Sam had walked into his own house and found his mum blind drunk. Until tonight it would have been hard to imagine his round and cheerful mother getting into that state. A glass or two more than was strictly sensible on New Year's Eve was quite normal for her; sometimes at family gatherings both parents would drink more than they were used to and become unusually giggly and crack some truly awful jokes that only they found funny. But it was all good humoured – nothing he'd ever felt really ashamed or worried about.

And him? Once, after a party at a friend's house last year he had drunk whisky, been sick on the way home and had a splitting headache the next day. But he'd never been insensible through drink. Unlike Sam's mum tonight. No, he could understand completely where Sam was coming from, and he could kick himself for being so tactless and smug dishing out advice. But, he felt, he wasn't completely without experience of these situations thanks to Nicky, and his suggestions had been well meant.

As Alex had trudged home he thought more about Nicky. He wouldn't be surprised if she got into trouble again – she certainly hadn't seemed too happy over the weekend. Perhaps it wasn't so easy being adopted, even with parents like his who, he often felt, were more lenient with her than they were with him, precisely on account of her unsettled start in life.

These days she had these ridiculous worries about her weight – but then half the girls in his class did too if their break-time conversations were anything to go by. But why was she getting these menacing texts? Why were people messing with her computer profiles? And why was she suddenly rowing with Mum and disappearing off to her room at the slightest excuse?

She and Mum had been at it again that morning before they left for school – he had no idea what it was all about – but it had resulted in Nicky running back to her bedroom and slamming the door. He hadn't noticed her at lunchtime, which wasn't to say she wasn't in school. He rarely bothered to look out for her, but today he had made a special effort, and had seen no sign of her. He was a little unsettled to realise that he had no idea who her friends in school were – or indeed if she had any these days.

He hadn't thought about it before, but then, looking for her, he realised there wasn't a single girl from her year group that he recognised as a friend of Nicky's that he could speak to. Maybe she was in a lunchtime detention? Certainly if her behaviour at school was anything like it was at home, some teacher or other could easily find a reason to impose one. Well, he decided as he went through their front gate and inserted his key in the front door, he could find out from her direct now what she had got up to today.

Or perhaps not! Both Nicky and his mum were in the kitchen, both very red of face and Nicky was screaming. His dad was standing, tucked away in a corner, looking alarmed and all but wringing his hands. His attempts to calm the situation had obviously failed completely and he had no idea what to do next. He shrugged at Alex helplessly as he saw his son stroll in innocently and then reel back when the full volume and ferocity of the row hit him.

Alex looked around him. Neither his sister nor his mum seemed to have noticed his arrival. He tried in vain to think of something witty and apt to distract them; wondered whether one of his trademark acts of clumsiness – like knocking a vase off the shelf – would help; and decided, wisely, that it would all be a waste of time. Instead he stood for a moment in disbelief – Nicky mouthing off was almost normal these days, but Mum in a state too? This was unheard of. He glanced back at his father who still seemed rooted to the spot, and then turned on his heel and escaped to the relative quiet of his own room.

Within a few minutes he heard the kitchen door slam, heavy footsteps as Nicky came running up the stairs, and then the slam of her bedroom door. Soon she had her music blaring. He opened his door and crept downstairs to the kitchen. His mum was sitting at the table crying, and his dad was standing next to her trying to comfort her. Neither seemed to notice his arrival, and he sat down at the other end of the table, puzzled at what to do next, but suddenly very hungry. There was plenty of the shop-bought quiche left over from tea still on the table and he cut himself a substantial slice and started to eat it.

Mr. Stevens looked up at the sound of Alex's knife clattering to the floor.

"Oh, hallo son. Had a good day?" He looked tired and troubled, but Alex admired him for trying to sound as if everything was as normal.

"So-so. What's happened?"

There was a silence. Mrs. Stevens looked up and her husband looked at her questioningly.

"Oh tell him. He's got to find out at some time or other."

"Right. Well, your mother has money missing. Quite a lot actually. She asked Nicky if she knew anything about it and, well, you know the rest."

"Oh."

"Yes. 'Oh!' Do you know anything about it?"

"Of course not. You don't suspect me too do you?"

"No. You see Alex, it isn't the first time, and we know where the last lot went. So we didn't think it was you."

Alex found he wasn't hungry any more. He put the slice of quiche down. With his finger he doodled absent-mindedly in some spilt tomato ketchup. He had no idea how to respond. Eventually he looked up and stared at his parents.

"I don't know what to say."

"No, I understand." Mr. Stevens really looked as if he did. "Anyway, I'm sure you've got some homework to do – why don't you go up now and get it out of the way."

Alex nodded, grateful for an excuse to leave.

"Anything you want me to do?" he asked as an afterthought as he reached the door.

"No thanks," both parents responded, and his dad added: "Everything will look better after a good night's sleep."

He had hardly closed the door before he heard his mum say: "I doubt that very much," and blow her nose loudly.

Much to his surprise, Alex settled quickly into his homework routine. Even with Nicky's music blaring he found he could concentrate and physics and maths had always fascinated him. He never could understand why Sam and others in his class made such heavy weather of such subjects – it was all so logical once you had a handle on the basics. He even had time to do the last optional question on the maths worksheet.

Finally it was done. He glanced at his watch – nearly 9.30pm. He was hungry again – and very thirsty, but he hadn't heard his parents leave the kitchen and he didn't want to go down and disturb them. Eating somehow seemed a rather tactless activity when there was so much tension in the house. He got up to casually examine his spots in the mirror hanging inside his wardrobe and gazed fatalistically at yet another crop just by his left nostril. Apart from looking far from pretty they would, he was sure, be hard and tender by tomorrow. Manfully he resisted the urge to squeeze them and contented himself with a few dabs of TCP.

Suddenly it was strangely quiet. Nicky had switched off her sound system. In the silence he heard his phone go – a text from Sam. He read it briefly and smiled. He didn't want to fall out with Sam, and was glad he had made the first overture to mend the rift. He went to text straight back, but in the continuing silence was broken by the sound of the front door slamming and, glancing out of the window, he saw his parents set off arm in arm. They hadn't changed so he presumed they were just going for a little walk down to the river and back to calm themselves down after the stresses of the evening. It wouldn't be the first time they had done that, he thought, re-assured. Why, they had been for quite a long walk last week after the washing machine broke down and leaked all over the kitchen floor and his mum's new shoes.

If he was quick he could get himself a snack and be back upstairs before they returned. And, he paused as he reached the door, perhaps he could get something for Nicky too. Whatever it was she had or hadn't done, starving herself wasn't going to improve matters. He wouldn't bother to ask – just go and fetch something that might appeal and take it to her room, maybe even eat his stuff with her - and her stuff too if she refused to eat it. The idea took hold as he sped downstairs and he completely forgot about replying to Sam until much, much, later – but by then he had far more problems of his own to worry about.

Chapter Eight

Downstairs in the kitchen Alex prepared a round of ham sandwiches and found a half full packet of digestives and the remains of a large family size packet of crisps. He also grabbed a couple of cans of Cola, remembering just in time that Nicky would only drink the sugar free variety. He piled everything onto a tray and set off back to his sister's room. He knocked and entered without waiting for a reply.

"Go away." Nicky was sprawled on her bed, hunched over her laptop and spoke without turning round. Alex ignored her and put the tray down on the table with a considerable clatter. One of the cans started to wobble and he just managed to catch it before it toppled over. Nicky still didn't turn round but her shoulders relaxed as she realised it was Alex.

"Oh it's you – you might as well come in then, seeing as you're here already. Did Mum send you?"

"Nope. She and Dad have gone out – for a walk by the river I expect. I felt a bit peckish and I thought you might be too."

"Nah, but thanks anyway. I might have a drink though." Nicky sat up as Alex opened both cans and passed her the lo-cal one. She also picked up one of the sandwiches Alex had prepared for her and nibbled a tiny corner before putting it back on the plate. Alex meanwhile had put a whole one in his mouth and was chewing thoughtfully.

"Go on, eat up. I bet you didn't have any tea," he managed to mumble through a mouthful of soggy bread and ham.

"I'm not hungry. Anyway you're not Mum so shut up. Not that she's my proper mum anyway."

Alex swallowed the last chunk of sandwich still in his mouth, "What do you mean? Of course she's your mum. Just like she's my mum. And I'm your brother, worse luck."

"No. Look at it Alex. You stand next to Mum and Dad and everyone can see whose child you are – you're tall like Dad and ginger-haired like Mum. Then people look at me and see I'm completely different – and they just know I don't belong."

Alex looked at her in alarm. "So? Hey, what's brought all this on? Not those awful texts surely? That's just other girls being bitchy. You've upset them by being so pretty, even though I say it myself."

"But look at me." Nicky was not to be distracted. "You are tall and ginger. I'm short and dark – like a little gypsy girl people say – even when they're not meaning to be unkind. And you're all clever whereas I'm ..."

"You're the best looking member of this family, that's what everyone says. Not something to be ashamed of I'd have thought. Boys look at you and like what they see. Girls look at me and have a fit of the giggles. See, I told you so, even you're laughing!"

Upset though she was, Nicky couldn't help smiling at Alex's words. Certainly her brother was no oil painting, though he did have a kind smile. Except of course he wasn't her brother – not her real brother anyway. She knew she had two of those older than her and Alex and adopted by other people, but she had never seen them. Did they think about her, she wondered, as much as she thought about them? What about her birth mother or, as Mum used to call her till Nicky said it was too childish, her 'tummy mummy'? Did she wonder about the baby she gave away?

There was silence as Alex ate another sandwich and finished off the crisps.

"You're one of us," he said through his last mouthful of crumbs. "Sometimes I think I hate you and wish you weren't here – but I'd feel that way about any kid sister when they were being annoying. Anyway the feeling doesn't last long – and who else could I have on tap to annoy if you weren't here? You might not like your birth family if you met them – especially your mother. She gave you up into care remember? I can't imagine Mum ever giving either of us away."

"Don't say that! You don't know why she put me in care. And maybe she wants me now – more than your mum wants me."

Again Alex was silent. He finished off the last of the sandwiches, including the one Nicky had started, while he wondered what to say or do next. Awkwardly, he put his arm round her, but she tensed and pulled away. He stood up.

"God, I'm not very good at this stuff – emotions and all that – but we do want you – love you even, whatever that means. Hey, I'm sorry, I seem to have eaten all your supper."

Nicky smiled. "Don't worry, I wasn't hungry anyway. I'm way too fat." She hesitated for a moment, and then turned back to her laptop, turning the screen so Alex could see it. "Look."

On screen he saw a web home page for *'soyouareadopted.com'* . Alex saw enough to see that it was a site you had to log into to get access, before Nicky turned the screen away from him again as she put her laptop back down on the bed.

"You're not signing up to that surely? Aren't you supposed to be over 18 to do that sort of thing?"

"Already have. I used Mum's card to join, and said I was 19. Don't look at me like that! Yes I took her card out of her purse, and I took some money – but not as much as she told Dad, and I intended to put it back after I'd had my pocket money – some of it anyway. But she noticed the money was gone straight away. She doesn't know about the card yet – that'll be another row I suppose, if I'm still here."

"Nicky!"

"No, only joking. I haven't got anywhere with this site yet, anyway. But I've put a bit about myself up there, so if my real mum is looking for me maybe she'll get in touch."

"And what then?"

Nicky shrugged. "Dunno. I haven't thought that far. Probably nothing will happen. I'm not expecting anything anyway. Just thought I'd sign up to see what's out there, and Mum and Dad made me so angry over tea, I decided to put my profile up there before I cooled down." She suddenly looked deflated and, to Alex, very small and very young. "You think I shouldn't've don't you?"

Alex slowly picked the last crumbs off the plate with a wet finger and put them in his mouth, whilst he tried to think of the best thing to say.

"I don't think you should've," he said eventually. "But I'm not you and maybe, if I were you, then maybe I would have done the same. I don't think it's right though. I think it all could get out of hand – you don't know what you've started. I think you should tell Mum and Dad."

"NO! Never! And if you tell them I'll run away." Nicky was almost screaming. She grabbed his arm so hard he winced with pain. "You must never, never tell them. Understand?"

"OK! OK!" Alex wondered why both his sister and best friend had ended up shouting at him that evening when all he wanted to do was help them. "I won't say anything."

"Promise?"

"I promise – but you must come off that site and de-register or whatever, before things get out of hand. Like I said, I'm sure Mum and Dad'll help you find your real mum when the time is right."

"But I want to now! Now is the right time for me. Why won't you listen?"

"I am listening. I do want to help. I just don't

understand that's all. I've promised not to tell. But you've got to promise not to do any more looking."

Nicky had her back to him by now. "Nicky will you promise?" He wasn't sure if she nodded or shook her head, but he didn't have the heart for further argument. Besides he could hear his parents coming up the garden path. His dad, at least, was laughing as they put the key in the front door.

"They're back," he said to Nicky unnecessarily as she could hear them as well as he could. He went to pick up the tray, but Nicky put her hand out to stop him.

"No, just take your drink," she said. "Mum'll think I've eaten then – at least that will be something to please her."

Alex nodded and straightened up with just the can in his hand.

"OK, but get that card back to Mum before she misses it, and for God's sake don't nick it again! Cheers, Sis." He waved the can in her direction as in 'farewell' as he went out and back to his own room. He closed the door and sighed heavily as he sat down at his desk and wondered about getting on with his homework. For once, even he found the prospect of extra physics boring, and his attention kept wandering.

'Damn,' he thought suddenly. He had just realised that within the space of 20 minutes he had agreed to be part of two of Nicky's deceptions on his parents. It was not something he felt comfortable about at all. But he was caught up in them now – he'd given his word.

Chapter Nine

Sam looked across the kitchen table at his mum who was gazing blearily at the grain in the wood of the table without, he thought, seeing anything. During the night he had resolved to have things out with her. His courage nearly failed when morning came, but he entered the front room briskly and tore back the curtains. Then, despite her groans, he shook her quite roughly till she woke up enough for him to almost frogmarch her upstairs to the main bathroom, pushing her through the door and then closing it firmly on her. To his relief he heard the toilet flush and then the sound of the shower. Some minutes later she emerged, still damp looking and wrapped in a towelling robe. She then crept down the stairs, to sit wordlessly across from him at the kitchen table.

While she showered Sam checked the front room and was relieved to find the 'sick bowl' empty and nothing worse than disordered cushions on the sofa. Alex had obviously been exaggerating, he thought with mild irritation. He opened the window to let in a little fresh air and took the duvet and bowl back upstairs. Then he went into the kitchen to make a pot of tea and toast. He was already late for school and had resigned himself to missing at least the morning lessons. Today he and his mother were going to talk – though looking at her now across the kitchen table - her hair wet, her hands shaking as she cradled her mug of tea and her mouth quivering – his courage again started to fail. He didn't think he could cope if she started to cry – at least not without bursting into tears himself. Steeling himself, he put his own mug down firmly.

"Mum, what's wrong?"

She looked at him briefly but didn't reply. Her eyes shifted back down to the table top with her uneaten toast going cold in front of her.

"Mum, we've got to talk. You're ill – and it can't

just be Dad going. I know you're upset about that – I'm upset too..." He felt his voice quaver and swallowed several times before starting again, more roughly.

"It's not helping anyone you carrying on like this – the drink and everything. You're not looking after yourself and you're not looking after me either. It's as if you're not my mum anymore." He felt himself really starting to cry now. This was not how he had intended this conversation to go, but she was just sitting there motionless, not reacting to anything he said. He felt it was hopeless trying to get through. He stood up scraping back his chair and thumping his fist on the table angrily. This time she winced and put her hand to her head. "No, it's not like that..."

"Well what is it like then? I'm doing everything round here and you're just like a zombie. I haven't gone into school today 'cos I was worried about you. And now you're up and we really, really, need to talk and you're just blanking me." He pushed the table away from him, making the plates rattle and his half-drunk mug of tea topple. He watched the stream of tea snake across the table and onto the floor.

"Oh, shit – now look what you've made me do!" He reached for the kitchen paper and mopped the table and floor, whilst his mum sat motionless. Then she started to cry – great ugly heaving sobs. He stared at her in horror.

"Mum! Don't!" But it was no use. She just sobbed more loudly and he stood as if frozen to the spot, damp tissues still clutched in his hand.

He was appalled. What had he unleashed? Should he get help? The doctor? Dad? A neighbour? Gran? Each suggestion was met with a shudder and louder crying. Eventually he turned and ran. School was out of the question, but he couldn't stay in the house a moment longer. He couldn't handle it. He felt he was going to explode. He kicked the front gate savagely as he went through and, hearing the satisfying crunch of splintering wood, didn't mind the painful jar to his toes through his school shoes. As he ran down the pavement he thumped each tree along the avenue with his right arm, enjoying the sharp jab of pain each thwack sent up into his shoulder. At least the pain distracted him from thinking – thinking hurt much more.

He crossed the road without looking out for, or caring about, the oncoming traffic. The squeal of brakes and tooting as he tore across, dodging between cars, gave him some grim satisfaction. On he raced, continuing right across town, past the normal turn-off towards school and on towards the retail park on the other side of town. Here he paused – more because by now he was exhausted, rather than the fact that he had arrived at where he wanted to be. In fact he looked around, panting slightly, in some amazement at where he was, and how far he had come without thinking about his movements.

Although it was quite a cold November day he felt warm from his exertions. He also didn't feel like crying any more. Instead he was angry – with his mum for being so pathetic, with his dad for not being there to sort it all out, with Alex for not getting back to him – they could have talked about how to handle stuff if Alex had have rung last night. Then he wouldn't have made such a hash of it. Most of all he was angry with himself – he was the one who had messed up everything this morning. What made him think he would get any sense out of his mother when she was in that state? Only his desperate need for some answers; and for a change for the better. But it was the wrong time, so he had achieved worse than nothing - and now he was going to get into trouble if he turned up in school late, without his homework, and not in the proper uniform. Three reasons for detention straight off.

Also he was starving. As he recovered his breath and calmed down he realised the cause of the nagging sick feeling in the pit of his stomach. He had not managed to eat anything before sitting his mum down at the kitchen table. And once they had started to talk - he winced at the word that hardly covered their non-communication - he had become too worked up to eat. Now, as he cooled down and the wind cut through his thin shirt, he realised that he was both hungry and thirsty – and that he had no money.

He couldn't go home – not yet anyway, and he certainly couldn't go to school. There was only one thing for it: he turned and set off slowly back towards the town centre.

Chapter Ten

The One-Stop was unusually busy when Sam sauntered in. Mothers who had dropped their children off at the nearby primary school and needed a few items before returning home; and one or two elderly people who regularly came in after the rush of people getting to work to pick up their newspaper and maybe a pint of milk. Sam was glad of this. He had no money on him, and no jacket either under which to conceal stuff. Only his trouser pockets. He wandered, with affected nonchalance, into the refrigerated section and, after carefully glancing over his shoulder to check he was unobserved, tucked a Ginsters steak and peppered slice into his left hand pocket. That should take the edge off his hunger. Now all he needed was a drink. To get to the soft drinks he had to pass the alcohol section – at least those bottles that the shop didn't feel needed to be kept safe behind the counter. 'So, no whisky or other spirits here then,' he noticed. But there were bottles of port and sherry.

Was this where Mum bought her bottles, he wondered. He thought he recognised the label on one. He looked at them with distaste – he certainly didn't fancy a sherry on an empty stomach, and wondered how his mum, with her slight frame, could cope – badly as he remembered. He blinked several times and shivered as he remembered the state she had been in last night, and the fact that she was little better this morning. It was horrible – the harder he tried not to think of the scene at home this morning the more vivid it became. He blinked again, partly to stop the tears that had started to well up, partly to get rid of the picture of his mum, mute and pathetic, the other side of the table. It was just too painful. He would have to deaden the pain or it would drive him mad.

Looking closer at the shelf he noticed someone had put a small selection of half bottles of Jack Daniel's there.

They should be behind the counter surely? He looked again. Leaving them out like that was just asking for trouble. He clenched his right fist to stop himself reaching out and as he did so felt a sharp pain in his right arm. He looked at his arm and was surprised to see his sleeve was all bloodstained. Of course! He had smashed into trees as he ran along to deaden the pain in his head. Now the pain was in his arm, and he needed something to deaden that pain. He looked again at the small row of bottles. Why not? Without looking round he reached out and swiftly placed one of the small bottles in his other trouser pocket. It just about went in.

"Oi! You! What do you think you are doing?"

The shop had emptied during the time Sam was there and it was now only him and the shop assistant. He was a large burly man that Sam had not seen before. He was advancing from the counter towards the drinks aisle. Sam didn't stop to explain himself. He was out through the door and again running as fast as he could, the shout of: "Stop thief, someone stop him..." falling away behind him.

This time he avoided the trees, but held on firmly to the bottle. The scare had given an edge to his thirst. He would get away, eat the pie and take a swig of the spirit. Then he'd feel better and be able to think straight. 'What on earth am I going to do after that?' a small, anxious, voice inside his head kept asking repeatedly. 'I'll decide when I've had something to eat and drink,' another, firmer, voice inside him replied as he carried on running until, with some surprise, he found he'd reached the river.

There was no-one following him now, no shouts to stop the thief. He slowed to walking pace. He knew this part of the river well – round the next bend were the boathouses his school used in the summer. They'd be locked now, of course, but at least one had an alcove. He could sit there out of the chilly breeze and the slight drizzle that had started while he was in the shop and which he felt at any minute was going to turn into proper rain. Now he'd slowed down he could feel how cold it really was, especially for someone with no jacket, and whose shirt was gripping clammily to his bare skin. He shivered. He was cold and hungry. But at least he didn't feel he was a hunted man any more. It was time for him to sit and eat.

It didn't take him long to reach the boathouses and he selected the one with a small alcove that was sheltered from the wind and the rain. The floor was covered in dry leaves and he burrowed a small seat for himself with leaves behind him as a backrest against the boathouse door. It wasn't very comfortable and he felt alone and miserable, but at least he could eat and drink here in peace. Perhaps then he'd feel better. With a sigh he took out his pie, tore at the wrapper with his teeth and bit into it. It tasted great.

Still chewing, he took out the bottle of spirits, unscrewed the lid, put the bottle to his lips and took a large swig. It hit the back of his throat like hot coals, causing him to gag up pieces of half-chewed pie, and making his eyes water. But some of the liquid made it down his throat and, when he had stopped spluttering, he found a warm tingle creeping all over his body. That felt good too! He raised the bottle again, taking a more circumspect mouthful this time so he coughed a lot less as the drink went down. Again he relished the warmth the liquid created inside him, and he started to relax. Was this what Mum felt? Is this why she had started drinking? He took another swig, following it this time with a mouthful of food. Then again, and again.

After ten minutes or so he looked at the bottle and was surprised to see there was only about an inch of liquid left. He was amazed – he'd never drunk that amount of alcohol in one go in his life – and this was strong stuff – must be 40% proof at least. He tried to check this on the label, but found it hard to focus. He was very tired and felt his sleepless night and eventful morning was catching up on him. It was, he decided, hardly worth keeping the rest of the drink – he didn't want to be carrying a three-quarters empty bottle around with him like a wino. He swallowed what remained in one go, again coughing as it was rather more than he had thought.

Queasiness came over him too with the last cough and he could feel himself wanting to throw up. He swallowed hard to stop himself being sick. He knew without trying that he would not be able to get up. 'If I just sit here quietly for a few minutes,' he thought, 'I'll feel better. I'll go home then and have a shower – much too dirty to go to school now. Yes, home and clean up, that's what I'll do. Once I've got my balance back.'

He settled back on the leaves and closed his eyes.

Chapter Eleven

The two police community support officers had parked their bikes and were looking at the unconscious Sam.

"Drink?" the younger one asked the other.

The older one, Julie, nodded. "Look, there's the evidence." She pointed at the empty Jack Daniel's bottle. "If he drank all that, he would be well out of it. Better check his pulse." She knelt down beside him and put her hand on his neck. Sam groaned slightly and shifted his body sluggishly.

"It feels about right. But his skin is very cold. It's nearly freezing and he's not exactly clad for the elements." She looked more closely at his sleeve. "Hallo, looks like he's been in some kind of scrape."

The other officer, who had been talking into his radio during this time, also turned his attention to Sam's arm. "Yes," he said in response to a question he'd received over the radio. "Lad about 15, dressed in what looks like St Faith's uniform – part of anyway. No he isn't wearing a blazer, or any jacket. Yes he has blood stains all down his sleeve. Yes fair hair. Seems well looked after, apart from the messy shirt."

He looked at Julie, who was regarding him with a questioning eye.

"They think he may be a suspect for a spot of shoplifting at the One-Stop in town. You know they always prosecute – or try to anyway – and they reported the theft earlier this morning, giving an ID similar to this lad's. Not your usual type of shoplifter though is he?"

Julie laughed shortly. "Oh, James, you've got a lot to learn! There is no such thing as a typical shoplifter. Just because he's a grammar school boy, and goes to St Faith's if his tie is anything to go by, doesn't make him a saint. Though he does look rather sweet lying there doesn't he?

Whatever; he can't stay here, we can't leave him, and we can't take him anywhere on our bikes. We'd best get the police along with a car so he can be arrested and taken back to the station."

James hesitated and Julie went on a little impatiently: "Go on, call for back up. This is too big for us and we can't just walk away. It's for his own good too – at least down the station he can be checked out by the police surgeon to see he hasn't come to any harm through the drink. And, if he's lucky, get a hot drink while they get hold of his parents."

Julie knelt down again beside Sam, while James talked again on his radio. She shook him firmly several times. Eventually he opened his eyes.

"Where am I?"

"Down by the river, the school boathouses. You've been drinking haven't you?" She held up the empty bottle. Sam nodded his head, then groaned and held his head.

"Oh, God, I think I'm going to be sick." He leant over and started retching.

Julie jumped back. "Mind my shoes! And mind your clothes too, whilst you're at it. But it might make you feel better." She didn't say anything for a while, as Sam was violently sick. When she was sure he had finished, she knelt down again.

"Was it just drink? Or have you taken anything else? Like drugs."

Sam shook his head. "No, just the bottle – and a pie thing, Oh God, there's more..."

He leant over again and Julie, still concerned about her shoes, leapt back again. But it was only a small trickle from his mouth this time.

"Good," Julie said, when he'd retched several times without vomiting, and sat back up. "Better out than in. And better here than all over one of our cells which someone would have to clear up."

Sam felt alarmed and struggled to sit up. "Cell?"

"Oh yes! You're a suspect for a shoplifting in town. The police car is on its way for you. No, just stay where you are, you're in no state to go home as you are – whatever would your mother say?"

"That's just it! I've got to go home, Mum isn't well – she needs my help. I've got to get back to her."

Julie put a restraining arm on him.

"No. You're in no state to be any help to anyone at the moment. Just wait here sonny. It's for the best, I promise you. You'd give your mother a right fright if she saw you like this."

She motioned James away as he came across to help her. "Just sit quietly with us," she said to Sam firmly, but not unkindly. Sam looked at her and she gave his left arm a reassuring squeeze. "We'll sort it, but first we must get somewhere warm. I don't know about you, but I'm freezing." She squeezed his arm again and Sam, feeling sick, sad, and very sorry for himself, started to cry.

All three were relieved when the police car eventually arrived. Sam found himself bundled into the back of the car next to a burly police officer. He was grateful that they didn't feel the need to put handcuffs on him, and he hoped he would not be sick again on the journey. As the car turned, he saw the two support officers retrieve their bikes and set off up the river path, pedalling calmly.

The police car soon overtook them, but he dared not look round. No one had treated him badly. 'They're not a bit like the cops on the telly,' he thought - but he was still afraid that any movement by him might be treated suspiciously. Besides, he realised as his stomach lurched after they went over a road bump to slow the traffic in the park, he might be sick if he turned his head. Instead he closed his eyes. He was soon asleep again, and had to be shaken awake when they reached the station.

Sam started to sober up rapidly as he stood, cold and dejected, at the front desk in the police station. His head ached, his mouth was dry and, when he licked his lips to moisten them, he tasted the sick still caked on them. But above all he felt embarrassed and ashamed. No-one spoke harshly to him. Nobody needed to – he just wanted to get the whole business over with and go home.

Slowly he handed over the contents in his pocket. There wasn't much, just a tissue and the wrappings from his pie. He felt in all his pockets for his mobile and was worried at first when he could not find it that it must have dropped out of a pocket down by the river. Then he remembered: it was still on the kitchen table when he had run out that morning.

The desk sergeant took the tissues and pie wrapping and placed them in a plastic bag.

"You've been brought up not to drop litter I see," he remarked.

Sam nodded.

"No receipt though; did you nick it along with the Jack Daniel's?"

Sam looked up startled.

"I never said I...."

"No, you didn't. And we haven't asked you yet either. We'll come to that later. First I need a few details. Name?"

Sam was silent. He didn't want to say his name and provide the link to his parents. He wanted to spare them that, he thought. But also he didn't want them to know what he had done. One thing was for sure – he was never ever going to steal from a shop again. Or get drunk.

The sergeant tapped his pen on the desk. "I'm waiting."

Sam looked down; he couldn't meet the man's eye.

"Sam," he mumbled eventually.

"What was that? Sam?"

Sam nodded.

"Sam what?"

There was another long silence.

"Look son, we'll find out who you are easily enough without you telling us. We can ring St Faith's and find out who, answering to your description, wasn't in school today. Or we can..."

Sam was appalled. He hadn't thought the school or friends could be brought into this. He had done something stupid he never intended to do again, and soon the whole world would know....

"Rainsworth," he interjected quickly. "Sam Rainsworth. But please don't tell my parents. They've got enough to worry about. And anyway I'm 14 now, nearly 15."

The sergeant's expression softened slightly.

"Thank you Sam. That's a great help. But maybe your parents should be worrying a bit more about you! We're going to get the police doctor to see you – he's here on his rounds at the moment so you're in luck's way. But then, if he gives the OK, we're going to have to ask you a few questions – and we'll need one of your parents to sit with you whilst we do. So which one – what about your mum – is she at home?"

"Yes. No! I mean she is at home, but don't call her – it'll kill her. She's ... she's not well at the moment. You can try my dad, if he's in the country."

"What do you mean, 'in the country'?"

"He travels a lot, for work. But I think he's back today. Oh Christ, he'll kill me."

"No he won't my lad. Not while we're around. Chances are he made a few mistakes growing up too. I'm sure I did too in my time – and look where it got me!" He smiled at Sam in what was intended to be a reassuring manner, but Sam didn't join in. His dad never made mistakes – except for the big one of leaving home.

The sergeant stopped smiling.

"So, we'll try for your dad then?"

Sam nodded. He knew his dad's number off by heart, but the chances were, he thought, that his dad wouldn't be around and maybe they'd relent and speak to him alone, and then let him go home. He could sort the consequences then without telling anyone. Except maybe Alex. He needed to tell someone and Alex would be sympathetic, he was sure of that. But he wouldn't speak of it to anyone else - and neither parent need know anything.

It didn't work out like that. The sergeant rang the number he gave and Mr. Rainsworth answered at the third ring.

Chapter Twelve

Alex had missed Sam in school, but was not really surprised he wasn't in. He wondered how the showdown with his mother had gone – or was still going. Personally he did not think Sam was going to get very far; his mother seemed far too sad for Sam to be able to put it all right in one mother and son chat. Mrs. Rainsworth, he felt, needed proper medical help. That, or a good kick up the backside to bring her to her senses. Alex fluctuated between the two options, and was glad it wasn't his problem. Except it was his problem too, if it was making his friend unhappy and making him act out of character. Alex was still worried about the shoplifting, and again his feelings were confused: Sam shouldn't do it / Sam shouldn't be put in the position where he had to do it. Both arguments were right in their own way, he supposed – yet they were also not right. He was glad most of his morning had been made up of maths and physics. There, at least, he was dealing with certainties, and the answers he came up with were right or wrong – no grey areas.

He had spotted Nicky earlier in the lunch break. On her own, but at least she was in school. She must have caught the later bus, he thought, or perhaps Mum had run her in – doubtful this though, judging from the look on the faces of both of them at the breakfast table this morning. And Dad wouldn't have brought her as he always used his bike to get into the university.

He waved at her across the school yard and she waved back and gave him a small smile. Yes, she was OK. But she was also a genuine 'grey area' for him. He frowned. What on earth had possessed her to get onto that website? What was this going to do to Mum and Dad if – when – they found out? He would have to have another talk to her tonight. He frowned again. It was just the sort of thing he hated, all this getting intense and talk of feelings, and – worse - crying.

A tennis ball hit him in the face and he spun round, his cheek burning.

"Come on Ginger, you goalie or what?"

He returned his attention half-heartedly to the lunchtime game.

"Sorry, you were busy up the other end, my mind wandered. At least I saved that one!"

"Only a bloody fluke, 'cos your head was in the way. Honestly Ginger, you're useless. Where's Sam when we need him? Have you seen anything of him today?"

Alex, by some fluke, again managed to stop a ball penetrating the makeshift goal. But not without him falling clumsily and wrenching his knee. He got up stiffly, rubbing the offending joint, and was glad the bell shrilled out across the playground, putting an end to all conversation and - to his great relief - any further playground footie. The other boys gathered up the sweaters they'd used for makeshift goalposts and went off whistling and chatting. Alex followed behind, limping slightly and wishing he didn't have double French and English for the rest of the afternoon. He could do both subjects OK. He didn't have a problem with any subjects apart from PE and art which both required manual rather than cerebral dexterity. But languages, even his own, didn't grab him – not like a bit of complicated algebra. He sighed and hoped the afternoon wouldn't drag too much.

It did, but eventually it was home time. He made an effort to find his sister, and to catch the bus with her. His classmates would tease him of course – they usually found something or other to rib him about, especially when Sam wasn't around. But he was sorry for her, and wanted to show a bit of brotherly love. If this could be demonstrated sufficiently by sitting next to her on the bus, then he was willing to make the sacrifice.

So, on balance, he was pleased to catch up with her

in the bus queue, and together they had jostled and pushed their way onto adjoining seats. Apart from Sam, he realised, there was no one else from the school he would prefer to be with. Funny, he had never thought about it before.

Neither spoke much on the bus and they set off back to the house, from the stop where the bus had deposited them, in companionable silence. Alex's stomach rumbled.

"I'm starving!" he said unnecessarily.

"Oh, Alex, what's new? When are you ever full?"

"Not often," he agreed. "But I'm a growing boy – need to fill out a bit." He flexed his rather puny biceps exaggeratedly and Nicky laughed.

Alex looked at her. "What was that funny noise coming out of your mouth then?"

She looked at him in puzzlement.

"I was laughing at you, stupid."

"Oh, a laugh was it? Just, I haven't heard you laugh for so long I didn't recognise it."

Nicky laughed again. But her face became solemn again quickly.

"Perhaps I feel a bit happier today." She paused, and then added: "I had a response to that website this morning."

Alex stopped in his tracks, and successfully swallowed a gasp of horror. Things were moving way too fast. He hadn't really believed anything would come of Nicky's actions last night, that all she was really doing was building herself up to be disappointed, and that when his parents found out, Mum, and perhaps Dad too, would be shocked and upset. He really hadn't bargained for any kind of response – and definitely not one so quick.

"What did it say?"

"Come up and have a look."

Alex thought there was nothing for it but to do what she asked.

He was glad, when he put his key in the door, to discover that neither of his parents was back home yet. Perhaps he could look at what Nicky had to show and talk her out of doing anything more.

"Just let me grab something to eat and I'll be right with you," he said, heading for the fridge. He poured himself a glass of milk and cut off a hefty wedge of cheese. That and a handful of biscuits would have to do for now.

"You want anything?"

"No thanks. Well, a can of Diet Coke would be nice."

"One coming up."

He put the can in his pocket and, holding the food in one hand and the glass in the other, headed for the stairs, leaving a little trail of biscuit crumbs on each tread as he went.

Nicky was sitting on her bed, her laptop open on her knee. He plonked himself down beside her, and she turned the screen towards him.

"Look," she said.

Chapter Thirteen

S am's dad had just about finished his tea when the phone rang. He had been eating with a plate on his lap, idly watching the early evening news. He didn't really have much appetite. He had not long flown in from Mexico and the lunch on the plane, whilst hardly appetising, had certainly been filling. Besides, the bread left in his fridge from before he went away had felt a little hard as he made his ham and mustard sandwich and had left a lingering mouldy aftertaste in his mouth. At least his coffee was good – he didn't skimp on quality beans and, preferring it black anyway, had not run the risk of spoiling it with the slightly off milk he'd also found in the fridge. Before he sat down, he took a fresh carton of milk and some bacon and sausages out of the freezer so that they would be thawed and ready for a more substantial meal later in the evening.

He put his mug down reluctantly at the sound of the first ring, muted the TV, and answered with his usual brisk "Rainsworth".

"Mr. Rainsworth? Glad to have got hold of you. It's the police at Stanton station here about your son ..."

"Sam?" Ian Rainsworth was all attention now. "What's happened to him? Has there been an accident? Is he all right?"

"No, nothing like that. He'll be fine once he's slept a bit. Some of my colleagues found him in the park, dead drunk and without a coat..."

"Oh dear, that doesn't sound like my son at all. Are you sure it's him you've got there?"

"Yes sir. At least the young lad gave his name as Sam Rainsworth, and gave us this number to phone you on."

"I see. Thank you for letting me know. Well I won't take up your time asking how he got into this state. I'll be down to collect him straight away and take him off your hands."

"I'm afraid it's not as simple as that sir. Soon as you are able to get here, and the doctor gives the OK we need to ask him a few questions. We want to ask him about some shoplifting at one of the stores in town."

There was a long pause as Mr. Rainsworth absorbed this information. Not Sam, surely? He didn't think Sam had a criminal bone in his body. Someone must have made a terrible mistake. He gathered himself together, took a deep breath and replied as calmly as he could: "I see. I'll be there straight away."

He put the phone down and fell back onto the sofa, his hands over his face. He couldn't believe it could be Sam down at the station. But at the same time, deep down, he knew it was true. Sam had been unnaturally subdued the last few times they had been together. Sometimes he had looked as if he were on the point of saying something; then turned away. 'Just as I've been with him,' he thought ruefully. God, how he wished now he had talked more to his son, found out how he really was, told him a bit more about his own situation. Even if this had driven him off the rails, at least he would have known the reason; had a recognised problem to work on. He shook his head, reached for his car keys and slowly and thoughtfully got up from the sofa.

But why hadn't Sam asked for his mother to be contacted? Did he feel his father could cope better? Had they tried for his mother and she hadn't been in? Or had she refused to go to the police station? He doubted that. He knew his wife was not very robust when it came to difficult situations, but she wouldn't have deliberately refused to support Sam. No, the boy must have asked for his father for a particular reason. He took a small morsel of comfort from this thought. Maybe he still had his uses. Whatever it was he had to face at the station, he could handle it – and so could Sam with his support. He looked at his watch – he would be there in 30 minutes, traffic permitting.

***

"Your dad's on his way." The young police officer looked at the hunched, bedraggled figure, crouched in the corner of the cell bench, a station blanket pulled tightly over his shoulders. Sam looked up at her mutely and the officer noticed two tear stains that had made their way through the grime on each cheek. She felt sorry for the lad. Despite being very drunk and a crime suspect, Sam's good manners and air of desolation had been remarked upon by everyone who had dealt with him at the station. She wanted to give him a hug – tell him it was going to be all right. But she had just done her probationary training; she knew her professional boundaries, and kept by the cell door.

"The doctor has given you the OK," she continued. "Though I expect you'll have the devil of a headache tomorrow. When your dad arrives we can start the interview straight away. Meanwhile I'll fetch you a nice cup of tea, and I suggest you try to have a bit of shut-eye till he comes. Milk? Sugar?"

Sam nodded. "Thanks," he whispered. He had a splitting headache already and was really thirsty. Maybe the tea would buck him up. He really didn't want to cry in front of his dad. God, what a complete arsehole he'd been. He felt very ashamed. He wouldn't be able to tell anyone, maybe not even Alex. It would be the first time he had kept a secret from him, but it was just too embarrassing, and wouldn't Alex say 'Told you so!' when – if – he heard about the shoplifting? But then, why hadn't Alex responded to his text? Why was his dad no longer living at home? Why was his mum in such a mess? Why? Why? Why?

He felt again the confused anger he had felt that morning over breakfast, the same urge to hit out and hurt something or someone, himself maybe. And again tears of frustration threatened to burst from his eyes. He was glad when the young officer returned with the tea in a polystyrene cup and a few brisk words about cleaning himself up a bit before his dad arrived. He thanked her for the tea and took a sip. It was ghastly – and why on earth had he nodded to her offer of sugar? He never drank sweetened tea. But it was warm and wet and he finished it down to the bottom of the cup, even crunching on the last mouthful of moist tea-flavoured sugar. And he really did feel a bit more in control of himself by the time his dad arrived.

Chapter Fourteen

Alex stared at the screen on Nicky's laptop.
"That doesn't mean much. It just says they acknowledge receipt of your payment and believe they may have some contacts of interest."

"I know, but it must mean someone else with the same name has contacted them, looking for me perhaps. You said yourself there won't be many people called Hitchin looking for their lost mother."

"True. But all I think that message means is that they've got your money and want you to stay hooked. You'll probably get another message soon asking for more money for them to do deeper searches or something. Then what are you going to do? Nick Mum's card again? Or have you still got it hidden away?"

"Of course I haven't! I put it back straight after you said. But just in her bag, not her purse. So she thought it was missing and started shouting at me again. Then she found it and came over all apologetic and said sorry to blame me for everything. So we're friends again now, for a bit anyway. But I still want to find my proper mum."

"And you can – if she wants to be found. But not yet. You're too young."

Nicky snapped the lid down on her laptop and turned to her brother, a look of fury on her face.

"Don't you ever listen? I've got to find her. It's like a part of me is missing. And don't tell me to talk to Mum and Dad about it – they wouldn't understand. They're so nicey-nicey they wouldn't be able to think there was something missing from their happy loving home!"

She spat the words out with such venom Alex was taken aback. He had never questioned his parents' love for both of them. Of course they could be annoying, but that was parents for you. At least they were a damn sight better than Sam's parents, and a lot of others he knew about from school. That Nicky could see their niceness as a mark against them was a shock.

He sighed and got up from where he was sitting next to Nicky on the bed. As he stepped across the bedroom floor he tripped and, looking down, he saw Nicky's trainers that she had left just where she'd dropped them. He gave a slight gasp. "Wow Sis, where did you get those laces? I almost need my sunglasses. They're vile!"

"No they aren't. They're great. Mum wouldn't buy me new trainers so I thought I'd smarten the old ones up. Besides, I like pink."

"And some! They're so bright you could almost read by them. Has Mum seen them?"

"Not yet. She'll hate them of course, but why do you have to be so mean to me too?"

Alex looked down at his sister.

"I'm sorry Sis. I don't know what to say that'll help. If I open my mouth I just seem to make you madder at them and me." He paused, twisting the end of his shirt round and round with one hand and scratching his neck with the other. Nicky was just sitting there, looking miserable and crumpled and much younger than thirteen even with, he noticed for the first time, quite a considerable amount of eye make-up on. 'When did she start wearing all that stuff?' he wondered. 'And what would Mum make of it?' He shuddered involuntarily, dreading the prospect of another mother-daughter showdown, with the added 'You're not my proper mother!' accusations to spice it up even more.

He sat back down on the bed, his mind working furiously to see if he could come up with something helpful. After a couple of minutes he turned towards his sister.

"Please don't bite my head off, 'cause I'm only trying to help. Why don't you leave the internet search for a bit? No don't interrupt, hear me out. Leave that..." – he waved towards the laptop – "...for a bit, while you find out a bit more information about yourself. Check out what information we already have. What about that box of stuff from when you were adopted? Have you looked in that recently? Maybe there's stuff you've overlooked or forgotten about, like where you were born."

Nicky looked at her brother. "Well I know that! It's somewhere in Birmingham. But it's true; I haven't looked at my stuff for ages. It might be fun to look again. Not that I think there's anything that'll help my search, but all the same; it's part of me..." Her voice trailed off.

Alex felt a small wave of relief. It was probably only a temporary stall in his sister's search, but it was better than nothing. He smiled at her and felt another surge of protective brotherly love – an odd sensation he had never been conscious of before today. Funny he should feel this way, just as she was feeling she didn't belong.

She didn't smile back, and in fact a small frown passed across her face.

"But how would I get the box without asking Mum? She'd get all upset again and wonder what I wanted it for."

"She wouldn't." Even as he said it, Alex wasn't too sure himself whether this was true. He had been surprised at how rattled his mum had been recently by Nicky's changed behaviour.

"I'm sure she wouldn't," he repeated. "Or Dad, for that matter. But I know where they keep it. I can get it for you and you can keep it tucked away in here while you go through it. Then I can put it back and they'll be none the wiser!"

"Alex, you're wonderful!" Nicky slid across the bed and gave him a quick hug, making him blush. He pulled away, laughing nervously and scratching absent-mindedly at one of the spots on his face.

"Don't do that," Nicky upbraided him bossily, just like she did of old. "You'll only make more come!"

He stopped his scratching straight away. "Sorry Miss. I'll get the box now shall I? Before Mum and Dad get in?"

She nodded and he disappeared. Soon she heard the scrape of the loft hatch, the squeak of the ladder and her brother's clumsy tread as he climbed up to their father's neatly arranged storage shelves in the attic – the only tidy area in the house. So that's where it's been all these years! Funny she hadn't given it a moment's thought since looking at it with her mum for a school project about families when she was about six years old. It would be good to go through it again, but this time in private, searching for clues about her origins that hadn't troubled her as a happy carefree primary schoolgirl.

Alex quickly found the box and returned down the ladder, closing the loft hatch behind him. Nicky took the box from him gratefully, and he could see she didn't want him peering in when she opened it. He looked instead at the food he'd brought up. He hadn't touched any of it since he'd entered her room – a fact that astonished him. Were there really things more important than food?

"Hey, do you want any of this?" he asked, but he had already picked up the biscuits and his milk, assuming what her answer would be.

"No thanks," she replied as he'd expected. "Just leave the Diet Coke. And thanks Alex. It's just like you're a proper brother." She had a closed look about her, and her eyes were already on the box, so he wasn't sure if she was joking. But he clearly wasn't needed by her any more. He might as well go to his own room, get started on his homework, and then see if he could get hold of Sam. How had the planned talk with his mother gone, he wondered as he entered his own room. Were things going to be better for him now? And what else had he been up to all day? He took a swig of milk and followed it with a mouthful of biscuit. Then he started to text.

Chapter Fifteen

"Now then sonny, I think you know why we are here, but I'll just run through it again for the benefit of the tape."

The police sergeant looked over the top of his spectacles at Sam, seated next to his father on the opposite side of the table. He was older than any of the other officers he had seen that day, and looked stern and rather frightening. Next to him sat the young officer who had brought him tea. She too was unsmiling, but her eyes were friendlier than her colleague's. 'Bad cop / good cop,' thought Sam nervously and shifted uneasily in his chair. Beside him his father also stirred uncomfortably and cleared his throat.

The sergeant switched the tape on and spoke with practised ease:

"Sergeant Smith, collar number 371, with Police Constable Graham, collar number 930. It is Monday 15th November at 5.45 pm and we are interviewing Sam Rainsworth in the company of his father Ian Rainsworth. They have chosen not to have a solicitor present..."

Sam was sure he knew what he was going to be asked. And he knew what he would reply. Once the police surgeon had given the OK and he was properly awake, if a little sore-headed, the police had allowed him to spend some time alone with his dad. He had told him about the shoplifting that morning and the previous times. Once he'd started, he found it hard to stop, relief at letting it all out over-riding any concern he had about what his dad might think about him, or how he may react. He didn't care any longer – he just wanted to shift this burden that was squashing heavily on his chest.

His dad had been upset and angry – but not with him, Sam had been amazed to notice. Nor with Mum, for not feeding him properly. No, it was with himself; and

Sam, tired, hung-over, miserable and ashamed as he was, found himself feeling sorry for his dad too. Sam had worried at first about how humiliating it would be for a man as successful in business as his dad to find himself in a police cell with his criminal teenage son – but he could soon see that it was his shortcomings as a father that were upsetting his dad the most, not what Sam had done.

"I did steal the stuff, Dad," had been Sam's first comment when Mr. Rainsworth had arrived at the station. "I'm sorry, I..." He started to cry before he could get any more words out. Then he took a big breath, gulped and added: "And it wasn't the first time. I'm sorry Dad."

Mr. Rainsworth said nothing, just sat beside him and listened. After a short while, when Sam ground to a halt in mid-sentence, he put his arms round his son's shoulders to give him a big hug. Sam didn't resist.

"I'm sorry too," his dad said after several minutes' silence. "Your mum and I, me especially, we've got a lot of explaining to do. But first we've got to get through this mess. Tell me about it – we've got plenty of time. Tell me the worst and we'll face it together."

And, after a moment's more hesitation, Sam did just that. How Mum had gone to pieces, how there was no food at home, how he had started stealing, just to eat at first; how Alex had been with him, but wasn't happy about the stealing – and was no good at it anyway. This made his dad laugh.

"No, I can just imagine him falling into shelves and dropping everything, poor old Alex." But soon he had returned to looking serious and Sam continued and told him about his confrontation with his mother that morning, how it had gone so badly wrong and how he had run out of the house without eating any breakfast and without picking up his coat or blazer or bag.

How he ran – as far and as fast as he could – to get rid of the demons pounding in his head. How he ended up on the industrial estate on the far side of town exhausted and starving and had felt he couldn't face home or school. How he had gone into the One-Stop just to pinch something to eat, seen the Jack Daniel's, and thought 'What the hell?' and stolen it without a second thought.

"Maybe I wanted to be caught," he ended glumly. "Everything was spinning out of control."

"Maybe you did," his dad agreed. "In which case it worked a treat - and you've certainly paid a price for drinking all that Jack Daniel's."

Sam looked down at his bloodstained and sick strewn shirt and grimaced.

"I must stink."

"You certainly do," his dad agreed with him again. "But not for long – I'm sure we'll be out of here soon, and then you can shower and freshen up."

Sam – who had started to feel a lot better after telling his dad all about his recent crimes, and was relieved that he had just listened to him and not pried, dug for more details, or started to tell him off – looked worried again.

"That's just it. When will they let me out – won't they send me to a prison or something till it all comes to court?"

Mr. Rainsworth looked down at him. "Sam, I really don't know. This is all a new experience for me too. Maybe we ought to get a solicitor, I don't know..." He noticed Sam was looking more and more anxious so he stopped; then started again.

"Maybe you should just tell the police what you have told me – everything, not just what happened today. It's not something you want to hide and feel bad about for the rest of your life, so it's better to get it off your chest. Then, if it looks like we need one, we'll get hold of a solicitor. OK?"

Sam nodded.

"So, shall I tell them we're ready to speak to them?"

Sam nodded again.

"OK." His dad took a deep breath and shot a reassuring glance at his son. "Remember, we're in this together," he added as he pressed the bell in the cell, and they heard the heavy footfall of an advancing police officer.

It wasn't long before they were ushered into the bare, bleak interview room and told to wait for the duty sergeant who would finish his current interview and get round to them. Sam stared around him. There was nothing at all in the room, apart from a small rectangular table and four cheap plastic chairs, two each side of the table. The table was old, with a Formica top spotted with burn marks from stubbed out cigarettes – a relic from the era when people brought in for questioning were allowed to chain smoke if they wanted to. Now the only adornment on the wall was a 'No Smoking' sign.

The only natural light for the box-like room could have come through a small window high up the wall, but it was by now completely dark outside. Even though it was high up the wall, too high to look out of anyway, the window was criss-crossed with thick bars.

The room was lit by a single light bulb suspended from the ceiling. Without a protective shade, the light was harsh and glaring – throwing what little there was in the room into harsh relief. The walls were painted two shades of grey – battleship grey for the lower half of the wall, a lighter shade for the rest and the ceiling. The overall effect was severe and forbidding – even if he had been tempted to, Sam didn't feel he could lie or hide anything from anyone in such surroundings.

At least it was warm – almost too warm. The little radiator on the back wall was putting out considerable heat and was too hot to touch. Sam found himself sweating and, after being in there for about five minutes, Mr. Rainsworth felt compelled to remove his jacket and loosen his tie. Both were relieved when the two officers arrived with their recording device, a bottle of water and four plastic cups, so the interview could finally take place.

Sergeant Smith put the recording machine on the table and plugged it in. When he had finished he turned to his colleague who had by now put her notepad on the table and taken a biro from her pocket. After a nod from her he switched on the machine and lifted his head to look over his spectacles and straight at Sam.

"Now then sonny...." he began, and Sam, with some prompting from his dad, told him everything.

Chapter Sixteen

Alex was puzzled. He had sent two texts now, with no reply from Sam. Surely he and his mother couldn't still be talking? He checked his phone for the umpteenth time. Still nothing. The boys rarely phoned each other – texting was so much quicker usually – but he was getting seriously bothered now. 'Best try ringing,' he decided. 'Have a quick word with him – check he's OK. Then, I s'pose, I'd better get on with my homework.' An essay deadline loomed and he wanted to do well, and not just to please his parents. Difficult though it was to admit to school friends – even Sam – Alex enjoyed studying. He just knew he wanted to go to university. He would, he felt, be a fish in water there, unlike at school. Maybe even find a girlfriend - one who didn't mind the heady mix of red hair, pimples and gangly limbs. 'Dream on,' he thought ruefully, as he dialled Sam's number.

The phone rang and rang, but there was no reply and it didn't switch through to take a message either. 'Damn,' he thought. 'Something must be wrong. Or maybe he's just out and forgotten to take his phone.' Unlikely. Alex often forgot his, or forgot to charge the battery, but he could not remember the last time Sam had been without his. It would have been an exceptional day for Sam – just possibly he was out with his mother, taking tea in a nice restaurant whilst they talked in a nice grown up, civilised way about how they were going to rub along together better now his dad was not on the scene. It was just possible, he thought, and there was no way - for the moment – that he was going to find out.

He sighed. There was nothing for it but to get started on his homework. He was still hungry, even after snacking and eating Nicky's share too, and he hoped one or other of his parents would be in soon so that they could sit down and have a proper meal.

Thinking of a family meal reminded him of the last one, and the hum-dinging row between his mother and Nicky. 'What is it with families?' he thought. 'And why mine? Why now all of a sudden?' Perhaps it wouldn't be so bad tonight; at least Nicky seemed calmer. He hoped she wouldn't do anything mad, and reading through the contents of her adoption box would satisfy her for a while.

There wasn't, he decided, anything more he could do for either his best friend or his sister right now. Sighing again, he retrieved his exercise books from his school bag and, resolutely ignoring the rumblings in his belly, settled down to a fairly engrossing hour or so on the rise and fall of Hitler.

***

Three hours later, he had completed his essay and eaten an unusually subdued meal with his parents and Nicky. Not that he noticed Nicky eating much, but at least she was there, and at least she and Mum hadn't rowed. He went back to his bedroom and checked his phone again. Still no text from Sam. He dialled the number to ring again and this time he was relieved to find the call answered.

"Hi, Sam! Why're you ignoring me?"

"Sorry," a voice came back. "It's not Sam; it's his mother. Is that you Alex?"

Alex was startled. "Gosh, sorry Mrs. Rainsworth, I thought I was ringing Sam's phone."

"You are. He left it on the table when he ran... when he went out this morning. Didn't you see him in school?"

"No – I thought he was with you."

There was a pause, as Alex imagined that Mrs. Rainsworth must now realise from what he had just said that he knew all about her drunken state last night, maybe much more. He felt himself going red with embarrassment on her behalf.

"I'm sorry Mrs. Rainsworth, I didn't mean..."

"No, no. It's all right. Truth is I'm getting a bit

bothered about him now, especially if he isn't with you. I don't suppose you...?"

"No, I haven't a clue where he may be."

"Oh dear." There was a long pause and Alex wondered if they had lost the connection. Then he heard Mrs. Rainsworth breathe in deeply. "Alex, I was just wondering, no it's too much to ask, but if you had a moment, if you could come round, chat to me a bit, about you and Sam ...."

Her voice trailed off and Alex said nothing. He was too amazed at the change in his friend's mother. It was as if she was pleading with him for help. He didn't know what to do for the best. Would it help track down Sam? Did he want to be tracked down? Would he be furious to find his mother using his phone? But then, he hadn't had any qualms checking up on his mother's calls and messages. What state would Mrs. Rainsworth be in by the time he got round anyway – always supposing he did go round? It was one thing to lecture Sam on the care of the drunk; quite another to face the problem himself.

"Not of course if you don't want to," Mrs. Rainsworth sounded apologetic. "I shouldn't have asked, I'm sorry..."

"No. It's all right. I'll come over. I expect he'll be home soon anyway and I can tell him what he's missed in school today."

"Yes, that's good. Thank you. Oh, and Alex ..."

"Yes?"

"I'll be quite all right when you come. Don't worry about that."

"I didn't think ..."

"No, of course you didn't. I'll be quite OK when you come. But I need to know he is OK too."

"I'll be there as soon as I can."

"Thank you. You're a good friend to Sam."

Sam's mother disconnected at last. Alex switched

his phone off and let out a deep breath. This was a completely unexpected turn of events. He wished he hadn't agreed to go over – he wasn't sure he could handle it if Sam wasn't there. And if he was, would he really want his best friend poking his nose in?

Quickly, Alex reached for his phone again and tried re-dialling – but this time it kept ringing.

Chapter Seventeen

Sam and his dad ran for the car through the cold damp evening air. He couldn't quite believe he was free; he had expected to be locked up overnight at least, and possibly until he was grown up. He didn't dare look behind him in case he saw an officer run out of the station, waving another form and shouting for him to come back, they'd made a mistake letting him go. Looking sideways at his dad, he felt from the way he too was running and panting that he had the same fear. Already he was reaching for his keys in his pocket as if they were criminals making a quick getaway from the scene of the crime. Though Dad, in his smart Savile Row suit and shiny brogues, did not look like the criminals of Sam's imagination. The thought made him almost smile.

They reached the car without being stopped and Ian Rainsworth pointed his keys to unlock the doors. They both jumped in and Mr. Rainsworth fired up the engine. They took off out of the station car park going much faster, Sam was sure, than the 5mph warning signs, but slowed to join the traffic on the main road. Only then, it seemed, did both of them start to breathe properly.

"Thanks, Dad," Sam said for the umpteenth time.

"My pleasure," his dad replied. "No, I take that back. This evening has been one of the worst experiences of my life, and I never want to go through another one like it. But I was glad to be there for you – and pleased with the course of action they have decided to take."

"So, I'm not even going to court then?"

"No. At least that is what the officer is going to recommend. I suppose an inspector or someone higher up has to make the final decision, but he seemed pretty confident, you being a first offender and making a clean breast of it all."

"But it wasn't the first time – I told them..."

"It was the first time you had come to their attention, and I suppose they are prepared to take a gamble it will be the last."

"You bet!"

Sam sounded so choked his father took his eyes off the road briefly to look at him in the glow from the street lights. He saw a dirty dishevelled shell of his normal son, looking much younger than his 14 going on 15 years. He patted him briefly on the knee and then turned his attention back to driving. They travelled on in companionable silence for a few minutes, then Mr. Rainsworth turned the car up a side road and started on a different route from the one Sam was expecting.

"Where are we going?"

"Back to my place. I can't return you to your mum looking like that. You need a shower and a change of clothes. Even turning up swamped in one of my sweaters and jeans is going to be less alarming for her than seeing you in your blood and sick-stained school uniform."

Sam looked down at his shirt, as if for the first time.

"Oh. I see what you mean." He paused, then added: "Does Mum know?"

"Not yet. But she's left a message on my mobile phone. That's a first so she is obviously worried about you – though she doesn't mention you. I'll give her a ring whilst you freshen up. Then I'll take you straight back – unless you want to eat first?"

"Please! I'm famished."

"So, you're getting over your ordeal then?"

"Sorry, does that sound too offhand – it's just I haven't eaten all day except a rather horrid pie – and I sicked that up."

"I'll see what I've got in the cupboard – I believe I have some porridge somewhere."

Sam almost laughed. "That sounds about right."

Again they drove in silence for several minutes,

then Sam asked: "What does it mean, a 'final warning'?"

"I've got a paper in my briefcase explaining it properly. But basically I think it means that they regard what you have done is serious but, all things considered, not so serious it has to go to court. But not so minor either that they can just let you go without any punishment. So, if they decide on this, what will happen is your mum or I will have to bring you back to the station and a senior police officer will give you a formal telling off and warn you that if you come to their attention again you will go to court. You'll also have to see someone from the youth offending team – know what that is?"

"Sort of, a couple of guys in our form were caught nicking cars and they have to go and see someone every week and do community work – doing up a children's playground I think. Will I have to do that?"

"I don't think so. The idea of seeing someone from there is an opportunity to discuss any problems you may have and any help you may need to sort these out that will stop you getting into trouble again."

"I won't! Ever!"

"Easy to say. But it can't have been easy for you, Mum and me splitting up and all, and you with no one to talk to. Might be useful."

"Dunno, I can handle it OK," Sam shrugged.

"Like today you mean? Sorry, that was low ball. I shouldn't have said that."

Sam had turned a hurt look on his dad and was about to say something, but he changed his mind. Instead he closed his mouth and shrank back down into his seat.

"No, you're right," he said after a bit.

"Can't do any harm – and it saves you a court appearance if nothing else. And here we are," he added as he drove his BMW into his allotted parking space and pulled on the handbrake.

Sam had not been to his dad's flat before. When he

had first left home he stayed in a hotel when back in the country. By accident or design he had been out of the country on business for much of the first few months, so the flat was quite a new acquisition. They made their way up the communal stairs to the first floor and his dad unlocked his front door and ushered Sam into a small windowless lobby. This led into an open plan kitchen living area. Sam looked around him. The room was barely furnished – just a three-seater settee, an upright chair, a small coffee table and a TV – he didn't recognise any of the furniture – his dad must have bought everything new. Through an alcove he could see a small but well-fitted kitchen that looked clean and unused.

"The flats have only just been built," his dad said. "I'm renting at the moment. There are two bedrooms so you will be able to stay sometimes if you want. Come and have a look round."

They turned back into the small lobby and his dad opened one of the doors which led to a largish bedroom. Sam could see a bed and a suitcase on top, half unpacked. There was nothing much else in the room, but Sam noticed a wall of doors which he assumed meant fitted wardrobes. Next his dad opened a door which led to a room that was completely empty. "The second bedroom – not yet furnished," his dad explained unnecessarily. He opened the third door, and Sam could see both a shower and a bath alongside the toilet and washbasin.

"Take your pick – shower or bath. There are towels in the cupboard under the basin and I'll put some clothes that might fit you on my bed. Meanwhile I'll sort some food and give your mum a ring." He pushed Sam gently into the room and closed the door on him.

It didn't take Sam long to decide on a bath rather than a shower. He was exhausted and a long soak was very tempting. Remembering the fun of bath times when he was little he looked hopefully around the bath edge for a bottle of bubble bath. But no, clearly his dad was a shower man. He would have to make do with soap and a flannel.

He started to run the hot water as he stripped off his clothes, and looked in amazement at the grazing all down his arm. He had forgotten all about this and his deliberate seeking of physical pain to drown out the painful thoughts in his head. He realised, ruefully, that it hadn't actually worked as an anaesthetic to other pain – and that it was now going to be pretty painful when he immersed it in the bath. "Probably no worse than I deserve though," he thought to himself grimly as he stepped into the bath tub and lowered himself carefully into the water, wincing as the moisture seeped into his open wounds. But none of these, he noticed as he teased the dirt gingerly from his arm, was deep or in any way serious. The worst bit over, he ran the flannel over his face, and then lay back in the water with his eyes closed.

It must have been, he thought, the worst day of his life. Worse even than the day his dad had explained that he was going away as he had done something that had upset Sam's mother very much, and it was better that he left so she wasn't constantly reminded of it. What was it, Sam wondered. What could be so bad his parents could just split like that and not talk about it ever? Or if they did, he certainly wasn't party to it.

Why had neither of them told him anything? Why, as far as he could see, had his mum not spoken a word to or about his dad ever since he left? Just gone to pieces before his eyes? None of these were comforting thoughts to be mulling over whilst he bathed. Besides, he was very hungry and he could smell something that was far tastier than the threatened bowl of porridge coming from his dad's kitchen. Bacon? Sausages?

He started to get out when a thought struck him. His dad had said he had received a message from his mum that day. That must be a first – and his dad was going to ring her tonight in response. Maybe he already had.

Chapter Eighteen

Does she know?" Sam asked his dad anxiously as they set off in the car to take him back to his mum.

"Yep. She's not best pleased – but glad you're safe."

"How did she sound?" Sam wondered if his mum had been drinking before his dad rang. If she had, his dad wasn't letting on.

"Like I said, she wasn't best pleased. But it was the first time we've spoken in months, so that was a bit awkward too. Otherwise, OK. She promised to have the kettle on when we get there."

"You're coming in?"

"Of course, you don't think I'm just going to dump you and run off do you?" His dad paused, as if suddenly thinking of something. "Oh my God – is that what you think I've been doing these last few months?"

Sam's silence was enough confirmation, and they drove for some miles in silence. Then Mr. Rainsworth cleared his throat.

"How's Alex?"

Sam, lost in his own thoughts, was startled by the question.

"Alex? He's fine I s'pose. He never grumbles – never seems to have anything to grumble about except having to do PE. I'm sorry I bit his head off last time I saw him – was it really only last night? I should've texted him or something, only I left my phone at home."

"Well you can catch up before you go to bed. What'll you tell him?"

"About today you mean? Everything – eventually. He'll have a go at me about the shoplifting I expect. Don't know what his parents will think – perhaps they won't allow me round the house again."

"Perhaps. But remember his dad and I were friends at university – and neither of us were saints. Not that we got into trouble with the police, I hasten to add. And I can't see his mum wanting to show you the door, not if she is still the Cathy Stevens I knew of old."

"No. But then she'll probably want to talk to me about my 'issues' and quote characters from history or books – which might be worse."

Mr. Rainsworth laughed. "Good old Cathy! There are worse fates, mind."

"Yes, I could be locked up in prison – or a youth offending institution."

"Well, never mind that now – we're here and you need to go and reassure Mum you're OK and won't put her through this worry again. Hello, who's that?"

As Sam's dad drew up alongside the kerb outside the house, he caught sight of a figure just going through the front gate. A tall, lanky looking youth in a hooded jacket. He was having difficulty closing the gate as some of the panels appeared to be hanging loose. Sam recognised him instantly – and remembered with a sharp stab of guilt why the gate was broken.

"That's Alex. He's grown a lot recently – he's miles taller than me now. I wonder what he's doing here, he never just turns up."

Sam wasn't sure he was pleased to see his friend just now. He got out of the car and called to him before he reached the front door.

Alex turned. The look of relief on his face when he saw his friend made Sam feel bad about his earlier thought.

"You're back!" he exclaimed. "Thank God for that – your mum was so worried, she rang and asked me to come over. Well I rang you really, but she answered. Oh hallo Mr. Rainsworth, I was just explaining to Sam why I'm here."

Mr. Rainsworth extended his hand. "Good to see

you again Alex."

"Thanks." Alex took his hand briefly and shuffled his feet.

He was more convinced than ever that coming over had been a bad idea – if only Mrs. Rainsworth had answered Sam's phone when he'd tried ringing her again, and he'd been able to back out of it, he could have been safely up in his bedroom on his computer or something. Now he was here, and could see for himself that Sam was OK, he really didn't need to go in and speak to Mrs. Rainsworth. And seeing that Mr. Rainsworth was there and obviously intending to go in too, there was even less reason for him to stick around. He was puzzled as to why Sam was wearing a set of clothes several sizes too big for him – but he could wait for the answer until tomorrow, no problem.

He shuffled his feet some more, and picked nervously at the new crop of spots by his nose.

"Well..." he said at last, "...seeing as you're home now, I'd best be off. See you in school tomorrow?"

"Maybe. That is – yes! Sure." Sam replied. "Thanks for coming, but Dad's here... and Mum ... and..." His voice trailed off. It was all too complicated to explain on the doorstep. Alex nodded his understanding and, without another word, turned and set off back down the front path. Sam watched him struggle briefly with the gate and almost break into a run as he reached the pavement. He smiled to himself as his eyes followed his friend's rapid progress down the street. Poor old Alex – he would have felt as embarrassed as Alex looked if he had found himself in the same situation.

The sound of his dad ringing the front doorbell brought Sam back to his senses. He was puzzled briefly about why his dad didn't just walk in but then realised that, of course, he didn't see it as his house, and probably didn't have a key any more. It was Sam and Sam's mother's home now, not his. For Sam it was one more indicator that his dad leaving home was not a temporary arrangement. He could have just walked in himself of course, except that he had left that morning without a key, so they were both reliant on Mrs. Rainsworth answering the door.

She seemed to be taking an awful long time, and Sam wondered again if she had been drinking, and was now too woozy to get up and let them in. He still hadn't mentioned this possibility to his dad. So they just stood together on the doorstep and waited.

Chapter Nineteen

Alex slept soundly that night and woke refreshed and relatively cheerful at the prospect of going to school after breakfast. He showered quickly, donned his uniform and gathered all his books together before setting off downstairs where he could hear his parents chatting. He nodded good morning to them and started straight away on the toast and marmalade. As usual he was starving and a re-fuel was his top priority.

His mum glanced at him and a look of mock despair came over her face.

"Honestly Alex, can't you eat without your mouth hanging open like that? Maybe if you put less in you would be able to chew more quietly."

"Sorry," Alex mumbled through a mouthful of crumbs, though he didn't sound very penitent and continued to wolf down his toast whilst simultaneously tipping cereal into his bowl and adding a generous slosh of milk.

"Much on today?" his dad asked him cheerfully.

"Just the usual," he replied, adding: "I saw Sam with his dad last night."

"Oh?" Mr. Stevens sounded interested. "Not his usual day for seeing Sam, surely?"

"Nope. His mum told me he hadn't come home last night. She asked me to go and see her, which I thought was a bit odd, but I didn't know how to get out of it. Anyway, when I arrived Sam and his dad were just arriving too, so I came back home. Looked like his dad was intending to go in with Sam."

"Interesting." Mr. Stevens looked questioningly at Alex to see if he had more information, but Alex was now concentrating on emptying his cereal bowl.

"Has anyone seen Nicky this morning?" Mrs. Stevens asked, with careful casualness.

Father and son both looked at her and shook their heads.

"Must have overslept," said Alex.

"Well she can't – it's a school day. Honestly that girl...." Mrs. Stevens pushed her chair back impatiently and went to leave the room.

"OK Cathy, you stay there. I'll go up and give her a knock. Better still – Alex you go. Yes – you! You know your mum and I aren't exactly flavour of the month with Nicky at the moment."

Alex gave an exaggerated sigh, put down his spoon, and set off up the stairs two at a time. He thumped on his sister's door.

"Hey, Snoozy! Get up you lazy slob – you're late for breakfast." There was no reply, not even a grunt or groan. He put his ear to the door and, on hearing nothing, opened it slightly and listened again. Still nothing, so he pushed the door wide and looked right in.

Even with the curtains pulled together there was enough light for him to see that the bed had not been slept in. He gasped with horror and turned and raced downstairs shouting: "Mum! Dad! She's gone!"

His parents left their places at the kitchen table and rushed into the hall.

"What?"

"I knocked but didn't get a reply, so I opened her door and there's no sign of her. Her bed's still made."

Mr. and Mrs. Stevens didn't doubt his word, but both still felt they had to check her room for themselves. Alex followed them back up. Soon all three were in her small room which, despite the crush of their bodies, seemed strangely empty. Her bedside table was unusually tidy and the bed was even neater than usual, as if she had made some effort to tidy up before going out. Alex noticed that her laptop was still in its usual place, but there was no sign of her mobile. Mrs. Stevens opened the wardrobe door.

"Her parka has gone," she said dismally, adding as she leant down to scrutinise the bottom of the wardrobe, and then swept the carpet with her gaze. "And her old trainers."

She started to cry and Mr. Stevens went to put his arm round her to comfort her, but she pulled away. "No! This is all my fault. I shouldn't have nagged her, I ..."

"Don't be silly, of course it's not your fault. You were doing what any mum had to do."

"But she wasn't just like any daughter. She had some problems, and all I did was shout at her. I've driven her away."

Alex sat down on his sister's bed. He was appalled at the sight of his mum crying and his dad looked close to tears too. It was all his fault, not theirs. He sat fingering his face nervously. He looked at Nicky's bedside clock. If he didn't get a move on he would miss the bus for school. But there was no way he could just go and leave his parents like this. It would be a first – he hadn't missed a day in school since he started at the grammar, and he wasn't even ill! But he couldn't abandon his parents. They would want to find her and they wouldn't have a clue where to start. Maybe, he did. Maybe, thanks to his clumsy efforts to steer her away from tracing her birth mother, he had in fact shown her the way to her – or at least she would think he had in some way, and gone off to track her down.

His parents were still standing between him and her laptop, so he remained fidgeting nervously on the edge of her bed. As he did so, his foot banged against a metal box hidden under the bed. He didn't need to look to know what it was. He felt his face go bright red, and pressed his hands into his cheeks to stop himself breaking out into a howl of dismay at what his good intentions had brought about.

After several minutes had elapsed, his mum turned to look at him.

"Oh Alex, do stop picking at your spots!" she burst out, before collapsing in tears again and reaching for his hand. "Oh, I'm so sorry, I wasn't thinking, I shouldn't have said that. And now you're going to be late for school on top of everything...." Mr. Stevens gave her another hug and steered her gently towards the door.

"None of us is going anywhere till we've sorted what to do," he said as calmly as he could. "Now Cathy, first things first – go and put the kettle on – we've had a shock and need a cup of tea. No! No arguing – you go and sort that and we'll then work out what needs doing over a fresh cuppa." He pushed her firmly out of the door and pulled it shut after her, before turning to Alex.

"You think you know something don't you?"

Alex nodded glumly.

"It's all my fault – but I was trying to help." He too looked as if he was going to cry. Mr Stevens shook him gently but firmly by the shoulder.

"That's enough of that. Blaming ourselves isn't going to get us very far. Just tell me what you think you know."

Alex nodded his head towards his sister's laptop.

"There might be a clue in there."

Mr. Stevens looked at him questioningly.

"She was trying to trace her birth mother – I wanted to stop her, or get her to talk to Mum at least, but she wouldn't. I tried to distract her, and I may have given her ideas instead."

"Well, we'll look on there soon. I'm sure you know more than me about getting onto the sites she likes and this is not the time to worry about respecting her privacy – she may be in danger as we speak."

Instead of reaching for the laptop though, Mr. Stevens sat down next to Alex.

"There's something else too, isn't there?"

Again Alex nodded glumly. He reached under the bed and pulled out the metal box.

Chapter Twenty

Sam had assured the police officers, then his dad, and later his mum, that he would go to school the next morning. It was part of the 'deal', his dad had said, though Sam wasn't sure that was the word the police had used. He woke, still tired and stiff, and immediately started to worry about what would face him in school.

Would his dad or the police have been in touch already? Would staff know why he had been missing the day before? Would they know about him being held in a police station, and why? Or would it be worse if they didn't know anything and he would have to explain? No, he really, really didn't want to face school that morning. But he had given his word, so he reluctantly dragged himself out of bed on the second repeat of his alarm, and shivered miserably under a cold shower to wake himself up.

To his surprise he found a clean school shirt hanging on the hook on the bathroom door. He had stopped expecting his mum to do such things, but if not her, then who? Looking down he also saw his shoes neatly put together under the heated towel rail. She must have cleaned those too. Unless Dad ...? No, he'd heard his dad go last night, not long after he'd gone to bed.

His parents had talked over cups of tea for a couple of hours yesterday evening; first with him there, explaining things about their break-up that he didn't want to hear, but that he also felt he already knew. He'd been angry at first, accusing them of keeping things from him.

"Why didn't you just say what was going wrong?" he'd shouted. "I could have handled it. Why didn't you just say?" Both parents had looked at each other then.

"You're right son," his dad had said eventually. "We should have just told you. Mum – we – thought it was for the best. But we can see now, it wasn't. We meant well, we were wrong."

"We're so sorry," his mum added, wringing her hands. Sam calmed down a bit then.

"Well I'm sorry too," he said after a bit. "I shouldn't have got into trouble with the police and stuff."

Then, as the rest of the events of the day caught up with him and he started to yawn, they packed him off to bed – just like old times. He lay awake for a while, listening to the low burr of their voices, hearing them move to the kitchen to make more tea, and then back to the sitting room to drink it and carry on talking. He was sleepy, but felt he could never go to sleep whilst his mind whirred with the information his parents had given him.

So his dad was gay. Had been forever, but he had married Mum because that was what both families had expected as they had been such friends for years. And he had really loved her – still did – but not in 'that way'. Not in the way that could keep a marriage going. Not when he had met someone else – a man, of course – though it was early days yet. He still admired and respected his wife, he said, and was ashamed of the hurt he had caused her. He loved Sam as much as ever too and was just as upset that he had hurt him as well.

And Mum? It seems his mother had suspected it all along, but had never asked. Because, as she said, she just hadn't wanted to know for sure as she didn't know how she would handle it. Then when she did know for sure – well Sam had seen for himself how she had gone to pieces. She confessed she would still be falling apart except that this incident with Sam and the police had made her wake up and realise she had to pull herself together and sort her own life out.

She hadn't put it quite like that, but Sam could see what she meant. Strangely enough, the three of them had settled down and talked more in that one evening than Sam could remember them doing for years, possibly ever. He simply couldn't remember any family chats from when he was younger. Funny that everything should appear so calm and normal just as it was coming to an end.

Mum had even laughed as she told them about meeting Alex's mother when she was feeling particularly low and how Cathy Stevens had dragged her off to the library for what she called 'reading therapy'. She had panicked at the library and allowed herself to be persuaded to take out a couple of Virginia Woolf's books which Cathy had said were her favourites, and which Mrs. Rainsworth noticed looked quite short.

"But I read the first two chapters of 'To the Lighthouse' and was completely lost. I never did find out if they got there in the end. I did watch the film about her on TV though - The Hours I think it was - where she drowned herself by putting stones in her pocket and wading into the river. So sad."

"Is that why you had those stones?" Sam looked at his mother with sudden consternation. His mother looked at him, puzzled for a moment. Then she smiled.

"Oh, those stones! No, they were ones I picked up by a little stream in Corfu where your dad and I went for our honeymoon." For a moment the faraway, despairing look that Sam had grown so used to recently came over her face. "I intended to throw them out; throw them in the river as some kind of symbolic gesture, as it happens," She paused to smile wryly. "But somehow I couldn't. Oh dear! You weren't worried about that were you?" Both parents saw from Sam's face that he had indeed been very worried, and his dad burst out: "God what fools we've been! Seems like we've all behaved like kids – Sam's been the most grown up."

"Well, not very...." Sam couldn't for the life of him see how his behaviour that day could be regarded as grown up. But he was so tired and overwhelmed with everything that had gone on that he could hardly think straight, let alone argue. He yawned and both his mum and dad agreed it was time for him to go to bed, where he lay, listening to them moving about downstairs just like old times.

Now he knew why it would have to end. The conversation with his parents had made that clear. Sure enough within the hour, just as he had drifted off to sleep, he was woken again by the sound of his dad leaving the sitting room and muttering hushed thanks and farewells to his mum. He heard the front door open and then click gently shut, followed by the car engine starting and the throaty purr of the BMW engine fading into the distance.

Shortly afterwards he heard his mother's steady tread on the stairs. He let out a sigh of relief – she hadn't been downstairs on her own long enough to get drunk. The day had changed her too. He heard her open his bedroom door as quietly as she could. He held his eyes tight shut and slowed his breath to a rhythmic and steady in and out. He hoped she only wanted to check he was sleeping OK and that she didn't want to talk – he was too drained for that now. After a few seconds he heard the door close again, followed by the sounds of his mum in the bathroom preparing for bed.

He felt himself relax properly. Only then did he allow the tear that had been held in suspense under his eyelid to trickle down his cheek. Followed by another, and another. Anger, despair, shame, loss, regret – he felt he'd gone through every negative emotion that day and that now, instead of sleep, he was destined to re-live them all night. And why not? It was no better than he deserved. A bout of insomnia was a small price to pay. But he was too tired, and soon he fell asleep. He slept right through the night until he was jolted into wakefulness again by his morning alarm.

Chapter Twenty-One

As he entered the classroom, hardly more than five minutes late, the form teacher's face was inscrutable. "Sam," she said, looking up from her register. "I've a note for you."

Sam took it, mumbling an apology for being late. He sat down in his usual seat and read the note, then got straight up again. The school counsellor had made an appointment to see him first thing. Clearly his form teacher knew all about it as she merely nodded to him as he went to leave the room and said: "Don't worry; I'll let your next teacher know you may be late." Was she smiling or scowling at him as he left, Sam wondered.

He hadn't bargained on seeing a counsellor so soon. That he'd have to see one at some stage was inevitable – every student who got into trouble with the police had at least one interview. Most came out of these sessions laughing – apparently all Mrs. Rees wanted to do was talk about 'feelings'. All they wanted to do was get out of the room as quickly as possible – so the best advice was to make a few up to give her something to chew on so she'd let you go early and everyone would be happy. Sam felt he had too many feelings at the moment – none of which he properly understood or wanted to talk about with anyone else.

Still, bunking off school was no longer an option as far as the police and his parents were concerned, so he soon found himself knocking tentatively on the door next to the senior staff room where a makeshift label saying 'School Counsellor' hung lopsidedly. He sidled in through the door when he heard Mrs. Rees's warm Welsh vowels as she called to him to come in. It was, he noticed, a lovely voice – even if the counsellor herself was not.

Once inside her room, Sam was invited to sit on a comfy chair at right angles to the counsellor, with a small coffee table between them. Sam, completely lost for words, sat down and stared at her dumbly. She was about 50 or 60 he supposed – much older than Mum, but not as old as either of his grandmas. She had no waist to speak of and was wearing a smock-like dress to hide this fact. Her hair was dyed light brown, but Sam could see an inch or so of grey at the roots, and a crooked parting. When he looked away from her face to the ground, he saw she had on sensible low heeled shoes, and thick tights. 'What on earth...' he thought, '...can this old bat have to say to me – or me to her?'

He carried on looking at the floor until the counsellor spoke. "You're not the first pupil from this school to get into a bit of bother with the police, you know, and you won't be the last."

Sam nodded dumbly.

"You're not the first whose parents have hit a bad patch either."

He nodded again without looking up.

"You're not even the first, whose father has come out as gay."

Sam looked up sharply then. How much had his dad told the school? She held his gaze briefly until he looked away and returned to staring at the floor.

"Doesn't bother me," he said after a while.

Mrs. Rees said nothing.

"Doesn't bother me," he said again, more quietly, his voice almost trailing away in a whisper, "Except..." Again there was a long pause.

"Go on," the counsellor prompted him gently.

Sam found himself crying, and Mrs. Rees silently passed him a couple of man-size tissues from the box on the little table in front of them. She sat by him patiently whilst he blew his nose fiercely and mumbled 'sorry' several times into the tissue.

Eventually he looked up. "Oh, it's all so

complicated!"

"Yes," she agreed. "It is. It's a lot to handle for anyone. And you have a lot of other things to worry about – your place in the rugby team, your GCSEs. All the normal stuff of growing up. It's asking a lot to have to worry about your mum and dad on top of that. You've done remarkably well so far ...." Sam went to protest... "Yes, you have. Look, you've kept your place in the rugby team; you're pretty up to date with your homework. Most boys in your situation would have messed up big time by now."

"And me too now."

"True, you've had a blip – and the police and courts only give you one chance these days. I'm here to help you make sure it is only the one blip – and to see if I can help with any other part of your life. I can only help you if you want to be helped, mind. But at least I can put a structure in place for it to happen. Does that sound OK to you?"

For want of anything better to do, Sam nodded.

"Good." Mrs. Rees sounded genuinely pleased.

"We're only meeting quickly today to get things in motion," she went on. "Here's the plan: you come and see me twice a week, and we'll work together on how best to use the sessions. I'll sort the times when I've seen your timetable. Meanwhile you attend school – no bunking, not even physics. Yes, I've heard about that! Hand your homework in on time, and keep up the rugby – you've got a real talent there I'm told." Her eyes went a little dreamy. "My son was rugger mad too," she added. "He was talent spotted by the scouts for the Welsh team once, but he broke his leg in the next game he played and was never quite the same again as a player. Referees for kids' games now, back in Cardiff... Does that sound OK to you?"

Sam realised she was asking about 'the plan' - not her son's rugby coaching.

"S'pose," he said flatly.

Mrs. Rees nodded briefly and rose to her feet. Sam

got up too. She took him by the shoulder and gave him a slight squeeze. "I can settle for that, for now," she said with a slight smile. "I think that's enough for today," she added as she showed him out of her room. "I'll be in touch."

Sam checked his mobile for the time and realised he had been in with her much longer than he thought and had almost completely missed the first lesson. Time had passed quickly and he might just as well now go straight to the labs for the next lesson. Besides it gave him a few minutes to think about his meeting with the counsellor. He wasn't sure what he had expected, and he didn't think anything much had happened, but he did feel a bit better. He still couldn't see himself talking to her – not properly anyway, but at the same time he felt he wouldn't mind seeing her again if he had to. She was OK as grown-ups go - and she hadn't mentioned 'feelings' once.

***

It was lunchtime before Sam realised that Alex wasn't in school. This was a shock: Alex was never ill. Even when he had a stinking cold he preferred to come to school and spread his germs around rather than stay at home, and have a few days in bed, or play on his computer. Sam could never understand his friend's desire to be in school at all costs, especially as he was so clever that, in Sam's opinion, it wouldn't really matter if he missed a lesson or two. He had certainly seemed OK last night, in the brief time Sam had seen him outside the house. So him being away today meant it must be something major – he'd fallen down and broken his leg perhaps?

After mooching about for most of the lunch break by himself, Sam found a quiet corner and sent his friend a text. The reply was immediate and terse – 'Problems.' Quickly Sam dialled the number, and a rather breathless sounding Alex replied.

"Hello, Sam."

"Alex – what's up?"

There was a pause.

"You wouldn't want to know."

"Course I would – I'm supposed to be your friend."

There was another pause, so Sam went on.

"Come on, you can't leave me in the dark. What's the matter?"

Alex was maddeningly slow to respond, but eventually he said: "Nicky."

Sam gasped. "Not dead is she?"

"No, not that bad – at least I hope not. She's run away."

"What! When?"

"Some time in the night I s'pose. I went to call her as she was late down for breakfast and her bed didn't look slept in."

"What did your parents say?"

"They're mad with worry, of course. And they've had the police in. But the police reckon it's early days and she'll just come back of her own accord. I think Mum and Dad think that too, basically, despite the worry."

"And you?"

Alex again was slow to reply and Sam noticed himself kicking his foot impatiently against the nearby wall to stop himself from hustling his friend.

"And you?" he said again. "You don't agree?"

"Oh, I just don't know." Alex stopped again, before rushing his words out.

"Thing is Sam, I think it's my fault she's gone – and I think I know where she may have gone – but Mum and Dad won't have any of it."

"Oh," Sam wasn't sure what he could say that would help his friend.

"Anyway, I'm going off to see if I can find her."

"What? Now?"

"Yes – what if she is in danger and it's all my fault?"

"It isn't your fault, I'm sure of that. But Alex what good would it do – you're not exactly the world's greatest detective."

"I've got to. She's my sister. Annoying brat that she is sometimes, I've got to find her."

"When are you going, then?"

"Now – in fact I'm already on my way."

Sam thought rapidly. His own troubles still weighed heavily on him, but there wasn't much he could do to sort them in the short term. Alex, on the other hand, was in trouble at the moment and Sam was pretty sure he could help him, even if it was only moral support.

Cutting across his thoughts came the piercing ring of the bell summoning everyone in from the lunch break for afternoon lessons. But there was no way he could just switch off his phone and settle down in class.

"Hang on," he said into the phone. "Tell me where you are and I'll come and meet you. No, don't argue, I'm coming with you. You aren't safe on an expedition like this on your own."

Sam could detect the relief in Alex's voice as he offered one more very muted protest to Sam's proposal, before giving him exact details of when and where they should meet. By then Sam was already half way down the school drive. He looked round a little furtively to check no teachers were looking before walking briskly out through the school gates and breaking into a run.

'Damn,' he thought suddenly as he rounded the first corner. Yesterday he had promised the police officers and then his parents. And now it was scarcely two hours since he had seen Mrs. Rees and given her his word as well that he wouldn't bunk school. Yet here he was, doing just that.

Chapter Twenty-Two

Nicky was on the beach. She couldn't remember where, but she knew it was the first time she had ever been on holiday. Mum and Dad had taken a caravan, which was exciting enough in itself, but it was in a caravan park overlooking a small bay. A bay that was more of an inlet. Here the sea was so calm that much of the beach was covered in pebbles, but there were small patches of sand where she could use her new bucket and spade to build sandcastles. Alex, his friend Sam, and Dad had built an enormous sandcastle on the first day and had helped her put her castle-shaped bucket on top like a tower. When they finished she added the little flags that Mum had bought from the little shop on the caravan park. Then they all waited for the tide to come in, first filling the trench the boys had built round the big castle, and finally washing over the whole of their afternoon's work.

She cried then – not comforted by her mum's assurance that this is what the tide did every day – and that tomorrow they could come down and build another castle. The boys laughed – that clever know-all laugh of five-year-old boys when their kid sister was only just four, which had made her cry even more.

But Mum shushed them and they all went off to buy ice-cream which they ate sitting on the edge of the promenade, their heels kicking against the sea wall as the tide lapped gently on the pebbles below them. Then Dad blew up an inflatable canoe and she and the boys took turns to sit in it whilst Dad or Mum pulled them through the gentle waves.

Sam and Alex even swam a bit. At least Sam did. Alex sort of splashed alongside him doing what Dad called the doggy paddle. Nicky supposed this was because it was what dogs did when they went in water – they just kept walking even when their feet couldn't reach the bottom, and blew and snorted through their noses. Alex looked funny as he puffed and spluttered next to his friend and Nicky laughed. Alex just grinned when he came out of the sea, and shook the water from his hair all over her as if he really were a dog.

The next day they walked across the little peninsular to another beach. This was a big sandy one, with what Dad called 'rollers' instead of 'waves' coming in off the Atlantic. He and the boys went in quite deep with surf-boards and floated a few yards with the incoming water, but Nicky and Mum just ran in and out of the shallow water, and she threw a stick for a little dog that had joined them on the shore, which barked with excitement until his owner called him away.

Later, after a picnic lunch which, she seemed to remember, had consisted of fish paste sandwiches, crisps and loads of squash, Dad suggested a game of cricket. The boys were enthusiastic so she was too, even though she had no idea what it was. The bat, when it was her turn to have a go at hitting the green tennis ball, came up to her chin and was awfully heavy. If Dad threw the ball carefully she managed to hit it a few times and when the boys yelled 'run' she ran to the stick near where he bowled and everybody clapped. She wasn't happy when the boys hit the sticks behind where she was holding the bat, as then they shouted 'out' and she had to give up the bat to someone else. Sam, she noticed, was the one who got most people out. She also noticed that Alex didn't like being out much more than she did.

Mum didn't mind though and after a bit she said she was going back to their picnic spot to read in the sun. Nicky decided not to go with her; she preferred to be with her brother and his friend even if cricket was, in her opinion, proving to be a bit boring.

It was hot and Mum had coated them all - even Dad - in sun cream, and insisted on her wearing a sun hat. She didn't mind as she thought the hat was rather pretty. Alex had refused to put his cap on and she noticed that the tips of his ears were quite red. He was, though, wearing a T-shirt at his mother's insistence and, despite the sun cream, his arms were going a shade of deep pink. Sam was wearing neither a cap nor T-shirt and, like her, was going brown rather than pink. 'He's nice,' she thought absently. But he didn't smile at her like Alex did, or stop when her shorter legs meant she couldn't keep up with them, or hold her hand when she was scared.

By now she had been put to 'field', and she had to run after a ball that Sam had hit right to the rocky edge of the beach, which landed beside a small pool. She threw the ball back as best she could and Dad shouted 'out' so Sam and Alex, after a bit of an argument, changed places. No ball from Alex came her way and she was getting even more bored so she went back to the little pool and dabbled first her fingers and then her feet in it. The water was warm – much warmer than the sea - and the rocks were bright and twinkling under the water where the sunlight hit them. Looking up she saw another pool further along. Then another.

Soon she had paddled in over ten pools. She could count to ten, but she wasn't sure how many more she had tested. In some, she had seen little fish. In others, small plant like clumps were growing on the rocks and moving gently about in the water with the waves caused by her feet. There were pretty stones and shells too and she wished she had brought her bucket with her.

She was totally absorbed and had forgotten all about the cricket game, but something made her look behind her. She was surprised that she could no longer see the beach – she must have followed the rocks round the bend of the cliff. Ahead, all she could see were more rocks like the ones she had just clambered across, and another beach beyond – smaller than the one she had come from.

Suddenly the little dog she had been playing with on the sea shore the day before bounded up and jumped into the pool she was looking in, stirring up the sand that had gathered at the bottom, then, shaking himself vigorously, spraying her with cold water. She took a step back and laughed. The dog seemed to be laughing too, and went to shake himself again. Then his master arrived.

"Down Paddy, you naughty boy. You've made the little girl all wet."

Paddy stopped shaking himself and bounded back to his master. His master was old – like Granddad. He was wearing shorts and wet sneakers and had nut brown legs and arms as if he had spent a lot of time on the beach. He had no shirt on, but was wearing a large straw hat. He was carrying a lead for the dog in one hand, but he had nothing else with him. He turned to look at Nicky.

"I'm so sorry my dear – was he frightening you?"

"No. He made me laugh. And wet!"

"So I can see. What will your mum say? Where is your mother?" He looked about him and Nicky suddenly realised that her family were nowhere to be seen. She hadn't been afraid. She wasn't really bothered now, but it was the first time she had been away from all of them since they became her family - apart from when she went to nursery class. This felt strange and she too began to look around her. She couldn't see either of her parents, or Alex or Sam.

Almost immediately she began to feel scared, and started to cry.

"Don't worry my dear, they can't be far away – we'll soon find them." The man and his dog climbed up on a nearby rock to get a better view. He put his hand up to shade his eyes so that he could look into the sun and onto the beach. At this moment Alex and Sam came round the corner.

"Nicky!"

Nicky jumped. "Mum and Dad are looking all over for you – what have you been up to?"

"I was just looking at the pools," she said. "And playing with the dog."

"Dog?"

"Yes – look."

But when she pointed up to the rock she could see the old man and his dog climbing down the other side. The dog was running ahead. The old man turned and gave her a wave and she waved back.

Alex tugged her arm quite sharply: "Come with me quickly. How many times has Mum said you mustn't talk to strangers?"

"I didn't talk to him – just the dog." It was almost true Nicky thought as she trailed after him, suddenly tired. She was glad he and Sam had arrived. She'd be safe now, and soon back with Mum and Dad. Mum would scold her of course, but then she would hug her, like always, and give her some squash. And then it would be time to go back to the caravan for supper and bed. My, she was so sleepy...

**

When she opened her eyes she was in a bus shelter, which smelt of sick. She had no idea how long she had been there but the sky was still dark. There was light from the shop behind and from a nearby street light and she could see she was no longer alone. A man was sitting opposite her on the other bench. A large man, and even in the dim light she could see tattoos running up the pale skin on his neck and onto his face. In one hand he held a dog lead which was attached to a large, unfriendly looking dog. It was breathing heavily and slobbering. It must have been its heavy breathing that woke her up. The hand holding the lead, she noticed, had HATE tattooed onto it – one letter for each knuckle. In the other hand he held a can of lager and she could smell the alcohol on the man's breath from where she was sitting, mingling with the stink of unwashed clothes and body odour.

She shivered and held her bag more closely to her. The man leered at her. He took a large swig from his can, wiped his lips with the back of his hand, and put the can on the ground next to him

"On your own are yer? Runaway?"

"No! My brother is…"

She could see he didn't believe her and her voice trailed away.

"Lend us a tenner."

"I haven't got any money." Again she knew he didn't believe her.

He leant towards her and grabbed one of the handles on her bag. She screamed and the dog started to growl. Terrified, she leapt up, tugging at her bag. But he was much stronger. With one yank he had it out of her arms. The dog, still growling, pushed his jowl into her thigh. She screamed again and, abandoning any attempt to retrieve her bag, raced away down the deserted street, past the overflowing litter bins, the broken bottles that dribbled beer all over the pavement, and the little mounds of what smelt to her like sick.

Chapter Twenty-Three

I t was mid-afternoon so the train carriage was almost deserted. Sam looked across the little table at Alex sitting opposite him.

"Phew, that was a close thing. I must be really out of condition; I'm right out of breath," he said.

Alex didn't speak for a minute. He was panting, his face was red, and beads of sweat had broken out on his forehead. Looking at him made Sam smile.

"At least I'm in better shape than you! Now tell me – what's the rush? Why this train?"

"I think she's gone to Birmingham," Alex replied after a few deep breaths. "And I think she might be in danger."

"And you think she's gone to find her mum – the one she was born to, I mean?"

Alex nodded. "She's dead interested in tracking her down. She's been looking things up on websites. I tried to stop her 'cos she's too young – Mum says you can get help for that sort of thing when you're 18, but not before. Trouble is, in trying to distract her I suggested she should look up all the old papers Mum and Dad already had. She's looked at them in the past so they're not a secret, though Dad keeps them up with all his official papers these days. Anyway I got the box for her, and I thought that would keep her quiet – at least for a bit."

"But you don't think it has?"

"Obviously not! Thing is, she knew already she had an unusual surname to start with, and that she came from the Birmingham area. And now...." Alex stopped.

"Go on..." Sam wasn't sure why this would have prompted Nicky's sudden departure.

"Well, you've seen the local news?"

"Not recently, no. I've had other things on my mind." Sam thought of the police station, his talk with his parents and then his talk with Mrs. Rees, and winced. Things weren't exactly going smoothly there either.

"But you must have heard about that murder case? The one where the woman was murdered in Birmingham?"

"Oh, the Hitchin case! It was on the telly last night, but I didn't pay much attention – other things on my mind. Some kind of gang feud was it? What has that got to do with your sister?"

"That was her name before she became a Stevens."

"Jesus! So you think she's headed off there?"

"I'm afraid so. She's got photos you see of people called Hitchin who were supposed to be her mother and sisters and brothers. She knows she came from Birmingham originally. And the Hitchin lot in the news come from Houndsworth Park in Birmingham. I think that's where she's gone. It's a clue of sorts, I s'pose."

"But what do the police say? And your parents?"

"The police have just taken a few notes and a photo of her, but they reckon she'll be back home within 24 hours as kids her age rarely stay away for longer. Mum is convinced it's her fault for shouting at her for pinching some money so she won't listen to any other possibility. Dad tends to agree with the police and thinks I'm being over imaginative. So they are just following the police advice and phoning all her classmates to see if she is with them or if they know anything. Trouble with that is I don't think she's actually got any particular friends in school at the moment."

Sam ran his fingers through his hair, started to speak and then fell silent as he took in what Alex was saying.

"You don't believe me either?"

"Yes, I do. If what you say is right she could well be in danger – they don't sound a very good family to get involved with. And we'll be in danger too if we track down the same people and find her there."

"You don't have to come if you're worried."

"Don't be daft! You can't be let loose on something like this on your own – someone's got to come along and look after you!"

"Thanks a bundle!"

Alex was looking anxious. Sam leant across the table and placed both hands on his friend's shoulders.

"Believe me, I'm with you 100% on this. What's the plan?"

Alex looked even more anxious. "I haven't got one yet – not beyond getting to Houndsworth Park and just looking for her. Once I realised no one was listening to me, I sort of panicked. I just felt I had to do something to find her."

"OK," Sam wracked his brain for ideas. But having plans was Alex's department, not his. "Let's start at the beginning: have you tried her phone?"

"Loads of times – she's just not answering – neither phone nor text."

"So that's not much help to us then. When do you think she left?"

"Must've been after 11.30pm last night – after everyone had gone to bed. And probably before 5am this morning, as Dad is often up and about by then."

Sam got out the timetable he had managed to grab when Alex was buying their tickets.

"There was a train at 12.02am that got into Birmingham New Street Station at 1.10am. You think she might have caught that one?" Alex nodded.

"But surely someone would have noticed her getting on at our end?" Sam went on. "Still, it's too late to check that out now. We could try the Birmingham end, but I 'spect the station would be more crowded even in the middle of the night. Not many staff about, so she probably wouldn't be noticed."

"Even if someone does remember seeing her, it

won't help us find where she's gone now, so I don't think we should waste time on that."

"True. Where is Houndsworth Park anyway?"

Alex shrugged. "Dunno."

"Well let's check – you've got a maps app on your phone haven't you?" Alex nodded.

"Do you know the name of the street?"

"Nope. There was nothing in the box about that. But I do remember them saying the murder took place 'near the centre of Houndsworth Park' - a 'Leaf Street' or something, so that's where Nicky may be heading for. I don't think she's been to Birmingham before – other than with Mum to shop in the Bull Ring. She probably has no idea that this Houndsworth Park could be a huge area of streets and houses. Possibly not a park at all."

"There's a school there. Houndsworth Park College. It's a sports academy or something now. We played rugby against them a couple of weeks ago. Rough lot – I've still got the bruises."

A train announcement cut across their conversation, telling them that they were now approaching Birmingham New Street Station. The boys got up.

"First, let's check my phone maps – but we'll need to get out of the station as we haven't got a good enough signal here." Sam nodded his agreement and followed Alex off the train and along the platform up to the shopping area.

"I'm starving," said Alex a minute later as they stood on the new concourse at New Street. Even in a crisis he was hungry. He looked doubtfully at the money he took out of his pocket. "I don't think we've got enough for food and for the bus fare to Houndsworth Park."

"Sorry, I forgot to take money to school this morning. Let's check where this place is – perhaps we can walk there anyway."

A quick glance at the map showed them that Houndsworth Park was to the north of the city – about two miles from where they now stood. It was a walkable distance and they were both very hungry. They exchanged glances and, without a further word, took themselves into the nearest station cafe.

"We'll be able to think better with something in our stomachs." Again Sam nodded his agreement as they both tucked into burgers and Coke.

***

It didn't take long for them to finish the burgers, and they took their half-full cans with them for the journey. Alex read road names out from his phone and Sam read the road signs and led them along at a brisk pace. After about a mile Alex said: "Right, we stay on this road for the rest of the way, almost. It takes us to a shopping precinct, and the actual park called Houndsworth is almost opposite." He crammed his phone back into his pocket and increased his pace to draw level with Sam, trying not to pant with the exertion.

"Thanks for coming," he said between breaths. "I don't know how I'd have managed on my own."

"We haven't managed anything yet – except bunking school."

"Oh yes – thanks for that too!" After a pause he added: "So, what happened to you yesterday?"

Sam was silent and Alex added hastily: "You don't have to tell me anything, you know."

"It's OK," said Sam. "Loads happened actually, but I'll tell you more at a better time. Basically I rowed with Mum, bunked school, stole some booze from the One-Stop, got too pissed to walk, got arrested, got bailed out or something by Dad, went to his place, then back to Mum – and now everything is fine!"

"Really!?"

"Yes, really. Well almost." Sam paused for a moment before saying in a rush: "Dad's gay, you know."

"So that's why...?"

122

"Seems so."

Alex hummed a little under his breath, fingered the spots on his face, then put his hand on his friend's arm. "That OK with you?"

"Yep, sort of. It explains a lot."

"You wouldn't be the first in the school you know."

"Funny, that's just what Mrs. Rees said. And you – what do you think?"

"Well, he's still your dad. He's still my dad's best friend too. I wonder if he knows."

"Isn't that what best friends are for?"

"Search me, I've never had one. Hey don't thump me! Look we're nearly at the shops now; we'd better check the map again."

Chapter Twenty-Four

S am's dad switched off his mobile and stared at it thoughtfully. He was both worried and disappointed. He had been so sure of Sam yesterday. Sure that when he gave his word to the police, to him, and to his mother, that he wouldn't bunk school again, that he really meant it. Only this morning, he was told, he had given his word again to the school counsellor. Yet here was the school phoning him to say he had left the premises without permission after the lunch break and that they hadn't seen him since. He had taken their family discussion so well! Seemed to anyway. All three of them had seemed more relaxed and settled after their discussion, and he had phoned his wife earlier and she had confirmed that Sam had been OK in the morning and had gone off to school no problem. She said that she too was OK – at least better than she had been for some time. For the first time in months he had felt he could relax.

So what went wrong? The school said there had been no obvious problems; that he had attended his session with the school counsellor and had then gone to all his morning lessons. So was the boy still deeply unhappy? Or was he just devious?

Mr. Rainsworth looked at his half packed suitcase. He was due to catch a plane back to Mexico later that day. But he couldn't go if his son needed him – and surely this truancy stuff was a sign of that. He'd better phone his HQ and let them know he might have to miss this next meeting – surely they could sort a contract out without him for once? Also, he supposed, he'd better let his wife know. Maybe Sam had gone back there and she knew already. He hoped his call wouldn't upset her and put back the progress he thought they'd made last night.

But who was he to be the judge of that? Things with Sam seemed to have gone wrong again straight away. He knew it was important to make these phone calls, but what he really wanted to do is ring his old friend Rod Stevens. He could do with a bit of sympathy for once – and good old Rod was always up for that. And maybe his son, Alex, would have a handle on what Sam was playing at.

**

Sam's mother listened to the two messages on her answerphone once again. First the school and then her husband – ex-husband as she must get used to thinking of him. She had no idea where Sam might be. Sure, he had looked tired when he set off in his uniform that morning, but he had taken his school bag and had thanked her for cleaning his shoes. She was pleased he had noticed – she was determined to be a better mum. But as she put the receiver down she noticed her hand was shaking. She sat down.

She could really do with a drink – but that was another thing she had decided against last night: no more drinking on her own. For one thing, it didn't in fact make her feel any better about her life. It certainly made her feel much worse the day after. Also it wasn't exactly a good example to Sam. Luckily she had no more alcohol in the house and she was not going out to buy any. Instead, she made herself a cup of strong black coffee.

Her mind kept whirring – where was Sam? What was he up to? Was it something she had said or done that morning? Her throat was telling her with every anxious swallow that a glass or three of sherry would help her sort it all out. 'No it won't,' she told herself firmly.

She knew she would have to find some other distraction, or she would go mad. She envied Cathy Stevens' solid calm whatever the crisis. Perhaps she too should read more? But not today – and certainly not those earnest intellectual books she'd ended up with before. Something to make her laugh; isn't comedy supposed to lift the mood? When this was over she would definitely try to read more, but at the moment what she most needed was someone to talk to. Someone who would listen, wouldn't ask too many questions, but could be relied upon for good advice. Yes, she decided, once she'd finished her coffee she'd give Cathy Stevens a ring. Cathy was always an oasis of calm in a crisis.

***

Alex's dad was at his wits' end. He had rubbished Alex's idea that Nicky had run off to find her birth mother, when there was a much simpler explanation in front of them – she had stolen from her mother and been found out. Teenage hormones had kicked in and now she'd run away to punish them all. That's what his wife thought and what the police thought too. And the police were pretty confident Nicky would be home before dark. After all, although she had taken her purse, she hadn't drawn any money out of the building society and her pass book was still in her bedside drawer. He'd also checked all the other bank cards and cash books in the family, but Nicky had taken nothing from them. So she was going to run out of money pretty soon if she was just relying on last week's pocket money, always supposing she hadn't spent any of it earlier in the week.

He didn't feel he could leave the house and distract himself with work, but he felt a bit useless just hanging around and waiting. His wife was busying herself phoning everyone in Nicky's phone book to see if she could speak to any of her friends' mothers, but Mr. Stevens could see she wasn't getting much information out of any of them; only a lot of sympathy and empty reassurance. How could these faceless strangers know their daughter would be back home before they knew it?

He had tried phoning Nicky's mobile several times, and he had left countless texts. But he had had no response. Finally, after a scratch lunch that no-one – not even Alex – had eaten much of, he went for a short walk to clear his head and returned feeling that it was time now to look more into what Alex had been saying about these adoption sites. It was still, in his opinion, premature and far-fetched, but listening again to what his son had to say was better than doing nothing.

So he went up to Alex's room – and found it deserted. He looked in every room, and went down to the bottom of the garden and called his name several times. No response. Had he just gone off to school without telling anyone? His dad was sure he hadn't – he had looked far too upset all morning, and was convinced Nicky's disappearance was his fault. Nevertheless Mr. Stevens returned to Alex's room. He found Alex's uniform in an untidy heap behind the door and his schoolbag next to the desk. No, Alex had definitely not gone to school. So where was he?

His wife was still on the phone, looking red-eyed and exhausted, so he wandered aimlessly into the kitchen. Both of them could do with a cup of tea, he thought miserably. Then he saw it: an untidy hand scribbled note from Alex saying boldly 'Gone to find Nicky.' Nothing else. Not where, or how, or anything.

Mr. Stevens sat down heavily. Now he had two children missing. Would Sam know anything? It couldn't do any harm just asking, and surely he would have his mobile in school – all the kids did these days. Of course he didn't have Sam's number himself, but Ian Rainsworth would have it. Sam's dad was a busy man with his own bundle of family and personal problems so Mr. Stevens didn't like disturbing him unnecessarily. But right now it was necessary, and he told himself not to be squeamish about giving him a call. What were friends for, after all?

***

Cathy Stevens finished trawling through all the phone numbers in Nicky's phone book. She followed these calls up by ringing the other numbers given to her by the kind and sympathetic mothers of current or, as she was quickly finding, erstwhile friends of Nicky. When the school day ended, she rang many of the girls direct. Not one of these, it seemed, was a particular friend of her daughter. None admitted to knowing if anything was on her mind; she hadn't confided in any of them that she was unhappy at home, or angry with her mum at all. In part Mrs. Stevens was pleased about this – but it made Nicky's departure even harder to understand.

Of course, there was this nonsense Alex had come up with about her birth mother, but Mrs. Stevens knew she had always been very open with Nicky about her adoption and was sure she would come to her first if there was anything bothering her. Wasn't she always willing to listen and talk and offer advice? She had often been a bit disappointed that neither of her children seemed to want this, but that was children for you – thought they knew it all already. Apart from this trouble with Nicky over the stolen money, and her obsession with dieting, she was, as far as Mrs. Stevens could see, a normal, happy girl on the edge of adolescence.

A new thought struck her. With adolescence came an interest in boys. Nicky had not, as far as she was aware, ever had a boyfriend. True, she had started to wear make-up and, Mrs. Stevens had noticed, would often go and re-touch her makeup and comb her hair if Sam came into the house. Sam didn't seem to notice, she had been amused to note. Anyway, the two had known each other since Nicky was really little – after all Sam had been on holiday with them several times when his dad had been away on business. There was nothing going on there surely?

But now the thought was in her mind she had to know. Sam's mother was a rather pathetic woman in Mrs. Stevens' mind. And she had gone to pieces when her husband left her. But surely she would know about Sam's whereabouts and, if Sam was home, she could ask him direct if he had any idea where Nicky was.

The chance that Sam would know something – that Nicky might even be in his company – was a comforting idea. In fact, the more she thought about it the more she convinced herself that Sam was the link that would lead them to Nicky. She could hear her husband bumbling around in the kitchen and hoped he was making a cup of tea – her throat was dry after all those phone calls. She ignored his shout of dismay – no doubt he'd dropped the sugar or something. Typical – any wonder Alex was so clumsy too, with a father like that? And where was Alex? Probably still in his room – it would be good to get him out and down for a cup of tea too, rather than up there fretting on his own.

Meanwhile she had this one more call to make. Everything would be clearer then, she was sure of it. She was about to dial the number for Sam's house, when the phone rang.

Chapter Twenty-Five

*W*here *the hell are you?*
Sam read his dad's text out to Alex. "Seems like the school must have noticed I'm missing and rung him up. What do you think I should say?"

Alex scratched his head and chewed his lips for a bit. "Dunno."

"I'll just pretend I haven't seen it then." He switched his phone off and stuffed it down to the bottom of his bag. Alex took his phone out of his pocket. "Oh, shit, I've got one from my dad too – do you think they've been talking?"

"Doubt it – they've both got other things on their mind at the moment. But we haven't got time to keep texting what we're doing. Why don't you switch yours off too?"

"Good idea. No! Wait! What if Nicky tries to get in touch? No, I'll leave mine on for now. Right, where are we on this map?"

Sam looked over his shoulder. "Obviously we are on the main street. The park is on the right, see? Just after that set of lights."

Alex nodded.

"That means the street where the Hitchin murder took place must be just off here to the left. Yes, see – there's a Liffe Street. That sounds a bit like Leaf Street doesn't it? Well, shall we go there first?"

Sam looked doubtful.

"Sun's sinking. If you think she might be in the park it's no use looking in there in the dark. What say we do the park first and the street after?"

"OK. But be quick. I don't fancy Liffe Street in the dark much either."

"Or here for that matter," added Sam. Both boys looked up and down the main street; the derelict and boarded-up shop fronts; the few open shops with goods – mostly fruit and veg, cheap clothing, or cheap hardware – spilling out onto the pavement; the betting shops with seedy looking men hanging about in the doorways; the boarded up pub. Sam felt very out of place in his smart school uniform underneath his firmly zipped up parka – and he wished his mum hadn't bothered to polish his shoes today of all days.

Both hurried across the road and into the park – which was surprisingly pretty and well maintained, though the abandoned boathouse by the lake was covered in graffiti, and there was a stack of empty beer cans and bottles as well as a couple of syringes piled up against the broken doorway. Sam winced, remembering his own exploits next to an – admittedly much smarter – boathouse. Who was he to feel superior to whoever had left this mess?

They checked out the boathouse and then went round all the pathways, looking in all the shrubberies. They checked out the surrounds of the deserted cafe, locked and boarded up for the winter, and returned to the gate they had entered by. Neither was really surprised that they had drawn a blank, but at least they knew for sure she was not in the park. "Alive or dead," said Sam, before adding: "Jesus, that was tactless, Sorry Alex."

But Alex didn't appear to have heard him, and was again digging his phone out of his pocket. They returned to the main street and paused briefly in the bus stop to re-check the street references.

"Liffe Street seems to run either side of the main street," said Alex. "I've no idea which one it is, but let's check out the one on the park side of the road first. It's a lot shorter for one thing."

"Sounds a good enough idea to me. Phew this shelter stinks – all piss and vomit and smelly tramps. Let's get a move on. What exactly are we looking for?"

Alex stood up.

"I'm not sure. Part of me just hopes when I get in front of one of the houses I will just feel it's the right one. But I know that's crap."

"It is unless you've developed psychic powers overnight. Surely, if there's been a murder, there'll be some sort of notice – a police warning sign saying something like 'Did you see anything suspicious?' And a date, and 'Please phone' etc., etc.''

"True," Alex agreed. "Or maybe a bit of police tape saying 'Keep out - crime scene.' Come on let's get going; it's almost dark."

The short stretch of Liffe Street they tried first, lined with neat terraced houses facing the park, gave them no clues to suggest the right house, so they turned and went back to the main road, crossed and set off down the larger stretch of Liffe Street. This part was a lot more run down. The houses were larger and looked, from the range of tatty doorbells at the side of each front door, as if they were home to lots of different tenants, with little interest in keeping the property looking smart. Each front garden was strewn with litter and there was a pervading smell of decaying wood, cats' pee, and rotten food. Sam wondered if he was being over-imaginative to think he could smell desperation there too. If Nicky had got this far, and this really was the area she had been born in, it would have been an awful culture shock for her. He hoped Alex was completely wrong and the police right – that Nicky had just run off in a strop, had possibly stayed the night with a friend, and was now safe at home having had a warm bath, a bit of a telling off, and lots of loving hugs from Mrs. Stevens - her proper mum.

"What about this?" Alex's urgent whisper cut across his thoughts. They were standing now on the opposite side of the road to a particularly dilapidated house. Several of the windows were boarded up, and one of the upstairs ones was smashed. The downstairs ones were still intact, but even in the half-light the boys could see that the curtains drawn across them were ripped and grimy. It looked deserted but, crucially, across the front gate were the remains of police tape that had obviously been cut through. The front door had wooden planks nailed across. The wood was strikingly clean against the rest of the building indicating that it had recently been added. This was the one.

The boys crossed the road and peered about tentatively. "It looks pretty deserted, but do you think we should try the back?"

"Do you honestly think your sister will be in there?"

Alex shook his head. "No. But I just want to make properly sure. Come on there's a way round the side."

Sam followed him doubtfully. Even if they could get inside, it was going to be pitch black in there, and they certainly hadn't thought to bring a torch. Maybe they could go back to the main road and buy one? But no, of course not! They didn't have any money.

"Oi! You kids! What are you doing messing about in there?"

Both boys jumped at the sound of the man's rough and angry voice.

"We were just...."

"Coming to gawp. I know. Just like the others. A silly cow gets herself murdered and everyone thinks it's a bloody freak show. We've had the telly and all, and now just loads of kids. Now piss off before I get my hands on you."

"I'm sorry," Alex sounded very middle class, in contrast to his surroundings. "I was looking for my sister."

"A bloody likely story! Well you won't find anyone in there now. Police cleared out all the hangers-on when they took the body away. Bloody disgrace, bringing the neighbourhood down with all their carry on. All those men..."

"It was a hostel then?"

"Brothel more likes! Bloody whores!" The man was getting properly worked up now. "And she was the worst; said she was called Betty Hitchin, mother of five, in the newspapers – I'd call her a lot of other things first! Say – *she* wasn't your sister was she?" the man cackled unpleasantly.

'No. But she could have been my sister's mum.'

Alex didn't say this, but Sam could see that that was what he was thinking. Sam had never seen his friend look so angry, or upset. He tugged urgently at his sleeve.

"Come on. There's nothing for us here now." Together they turned on their heels and ran back up to the main road.

In silence, they retraced their steps down the main street which was quite crowded now, with people on foot doing some last minute shopping on the way home from work and commuters in cars inching their way up the busy road, hooting impatiently as people tried to cross in front of them. Some of the pedestrians were in no hurry though, as if they had no work to hurry from – and no home to speak of to hurry to.

Among these was a large smelly man with a bad tempered looking dog and a surprisingly clean-looking rucksack on his back that looked vaguely familiar to Alex. He was lurching along, drinking from a can of lager and he swore loudly after the boys nearly bumped into him as he swayed drunkenly into their path. They ignored him and his dog, and pushed their way through the crowds as fast as they could, anxious now to get back to the station and get back home themselves.

Chapter Twenty-Six

As they trudged wearily onto the brightly lit station concourse, Sam felt he had never been so downhearted – not even yesterday in the police station. Was it really only 24 hours ago, he thought, that he and his dad were sitting across the desk in that stuffy overheated interview room? Only 24 hours ago that he had promised faithfully to attend school regularly and be home by 8pm every night? Well, he'd messed up the first promise and it would take a miracle – or an extremely fast train such as hadn't yet been invented - to get him home before the curfew.

'Damn,' he thought miserably. 'I'll probably end up in a young offender institution after all. And all I was doing was trying to help. Fat chance!' He looked across at his friend and seeing that, if anything, his friend looked even more miserable than he did, he felt a stab of guilt. 'Poor old Alex, he's taken us on this adventure to rescue his sister – and drawn a blank. Now he's got the worry of where she really is – is she safe? Is she alive even? And I'm just worrying about my own skin!'

Alex looked up and caught his friend's eye. "I suppose you think the whole thing has been stupid?"

"Course not! We didn't find her, but we're pretty sure she isn't caught up in that awful household. If she did go there and see for herself the state of that house and got an earful from that bloke about the woman who was possibly her mother, then at least she should feel better about living with you lot."

"If you say so." Alex was unconvinced.

"Well I do. I don't think the journey has been wasted at all. And she'll know how much you care for her when we do actually find her."

"When. Or if, rather! I wonder if she's home." He pulled his phone out and checked his texts and

135

answerphone. "No, loads of texts and messages from Dad wondering where I am, but nothing to say Nicky is back."

Sam found his phone, and switched it back on.

"Same with me – just two more texts from Dad and a phone message. Plus one from Mum. Oh damn it, they both sound worried – perhaps I should call them."

"Let's wait till we get back. We haven't got anything very positive to say, after all."

"OK." Sam was quite happy to postpone facing the wrath of either or both his parents. He switched his phone off again and stuffed it back down in his bag.

As they trudged towards the ticket inspection barriers, with the smell from tempting food booths offering hot muffins and pies assaulting their nostrils, Alex stopped to search for their tickets, found them at last, and looked up again. They were standing by yet another food outlet, this time stacked with croissants and mini pizzas. "I'm sure I shouldn't feel hungry at a time like this, but the fact is I'm starving."

"Me too," Sam confessed.

"You don't think you...."

"No!" Sam was adamant. "I've messed up just about everything else in my agreement so far. But the one thing I'm not doing – not even for you – is nicking anything, ever again."

"OK, OK, sorry I asked. I'm not really that hungry anyway." Alex added unconvincingly. "Hello, what's that huddle of police officers doing over there? Do you think they've come to arrest you for bunking school?"

Sam gave a start. He knew they wouldn't be there for that, but just now the sight of any police officer made him feel like a marked criminal.

"No, of course they're not," he replied shakily. "They're not all police either – seems like most of them are station staff. And there's something on the floor. That's what they are interested in. Come on, let's get through the ticket inspectors and see when the next train is."

"No. Wait!" Alex was looking more closely at the clutch of officials. "It's a body, not a thing – I think it's a girl huddled up – I can see her feet." He would recognise those laces anywhere. He just had to get closer to check them out.

He set off towards the little crowd, with Sam trailing behind reluctantly – he didn't want any more contact with the police than necessary at the moment. But he quickened his pace as Alex let out a whoop and broke into a run.

"Nicky!" he called excitedly. "Nicky – it's Alex!" He pushed his way through the officers and knelt down.

Chapter Twenty-Seven

■ ■ **Y**our sister, eh? Perhaps you could give us your name – and hers?" The police officer did not look as brusque as his words suggested; in fact he smiled quite kindly at Alex. "It's just we've been here for nearly half an hour – ever since the station security staff called us, and she's just sat there, not saying a word. Doesn't even seem to know we are here."

Alex looked up at Sam as if for guidance and Sam, mindful of his own contact with the police, shook his head slightly. He didn't want his name being taken down and reported back to the local police so they'd know he had broken his agreement the very next night. He shuddered at the prospect of being sent to a young offender institution with real criminals, and felt slightly sick. Alex turned back to his sister. She too was shaking her head, though whether that was in response to his unspoken query, or was part of a silent dialogue she was having with herself, he couldn't say.

After several seconds, during which the police officer had taken out his notepad and had continued to smile encouragingly at Alex, he made a decision. He, Nicky and Sam needed help, and as far as he could see, the adults around Nicky were trying to offer just that. From what he understood of police activity, if they had wanted to arrest her they would have put her in handcuffs and dragged her off in a police van to the local station ages ago. So Nicky clearly wasn't in any criminal kind of trouble. Sam of course was a different matter, but he would have to look out for himself. On this occasion his sister was coming first. He took a deep breath.

"My name is Alex Stevens, and this is my sister Nicky."

"Thank you. And the other young man?" The police officer turned towards Sam.

"He's my friend. He came to help me look for my sister, that's all."

For the moment, that seemed to satisfy the police officer. He crouched down next to Alex so that he was on the same level as Nicky. "Tell me, my dear, is this your brother?"

For the first time, Nicky seemed to register the people around her. She looked up at Alex and gave a weak smile. Then she turned to the police officer and nodded.

"And the other lad?"

"Alex's friend, Sam." Sam squirmed, but she didn't say anymore, so he too smiled at her.

"Thank God we've found you. Alex has been worried sick."

"And Mum and Dad too," added Alex. "It's just I had a bit of an idea where you might have gone and Sam agreed to come with me, to help find you." Alex thought back to the derelict house and the disagreeable neighbour. "Oh, Nicky – was it very awful?"

Nicky nodded. A big tear rolled down her cheek and she buried her head in her brother's shoulder, hugging him tightly. He put his arms round her awkwardly and gave her a slight squeeze.

"Steady on Sis," he said in a wobbly voice. "You'll get me going next."

All but two of the station staff were leaving now and, Sam was pleased to note, both the police officers were going with them. They clearly didn't see the problem as a police matter now Nicky had someone with her. One of the remaining station staff came forward. She coughed to try to attract Alex and Nicky's attention, but they were just hugging each other, oblivious to everyone else, so she turned to Sam.

"Now the young lady has her brother and is not so frightened, perhaps you could all come back with me to our office. We have to do a bit of paperwork to round this off.

But we could find you some tea, or squash, and maybe some toast while we're at it." This sounded like a good idea to Sam.

"Ooh, yes please. I'm sure my friend will be hungry too. He usually is, and now he's found his sister I expect he'll be absolutely famished again. Alex!" He called loudly, leaning down towards his friend. "The people here are offering us some food if we go with them back to the office. You probably need to eat, as usual. You must be hungry too, Nicky." He looked straight at his friend's sister for the first time that evening and noticed her grimy tear-stained face. 'Funny...' he thought, 'She seems to have come out without a bag.' In his - admittedly very limited – experience, girls never went anywhere without quite a hefty pile of stuff in some shiny bag or other – and that was where they kept their mobiles, not in their trouser pockets because, as his mother had explained to him once, it would spoil the 'line'.

Both Alex and Nicky shook their heads at the offer of food. Then Alex stopped. "No, now you mention it I'm starving. We can't have eaten for over four hours." He stood up, pulling his sister up after him.

"Just follow us then, we'll go ahead and put the kettle on." The station staff set off purposefully towards their small office in the far corner of the station precinct.

"Come on Sis," said Alex. "You'll feel a lot better with a bit of food in you. Then perhaps we should be getting you home."

Nicky shrank back suddenly and slumped back onto the floor. "That's just it! I was trying to get home, but someone stole my rucksack with all my money and my ticket in it. I tried to get on a train anyway, but the ticket inspector stopped me, so I came and sat down here whilst I tried to work out what to do."

"You could have phoned me, or Mum, or Dad," Alex said.

"But I couldn't, see. My phone was in my bag too!"

"You chump. Why didn't you keep it in your pocket?"

Nicky just looked at him, so Sam intervened helpfully: "Because it would spoil the line of her jeans."

Alex shook his head in disbelief before continuing: "Why didn't you tell the ticket inspector?"

"I did, but he just said: 'They all say that!' I could see he didn't believe me, so I didn't think anyone else would either."

Alex stopped suddenly.

"Can you describe who stole your bag?"

"Not really, I was half asleep, waiting for the bus back to the station. I remember he was big and smelly, and had a large unfriendly dog that growled at me."

"I knew it! I thought that bag was familiar! Remember Sam - that tramp who swore at us? I noticed he had a small pinky coloured rucksack that looked so much cleaner than the rest of him. If only I had known! There are piles of messages from me on your phone, and probably from Mum and Dad too."

"Well, too late now." Sam interrupted quickly. He wasn't keen on returning to the Houndsworth Park area, and it didn't seem that Alex was that way inclined either.

"No, I don't fancy tackling that tramp – always supposing we could find him now in the dark. I'm sure Mum and Dad will get you another bag and phone. They'll be pleased enough to have you back safe and sound."

"Should we phone them now?" Sam sounded doubtful.

"We must! But not before we've eaten something!" Sam was amused to see Alex had his priorities back in their usual order, and even Nicky allowed a fleeting smile to cross her face as the station staff held open the door and the three children went into a small untidy office that was almost too warm and smelt tantalisingly of coffee.

Chapter Twenty-Eight

■ ■ "Good of them to phone the parents for us. Sort out all the awkward questions and stuff." Sam looked at Alex and Nicky seated opposite him on the train home. Both nodded.

"Good of them to give me a free ticket – at least someone believed me when I said I'd lost it," Nicky murmured. The boys nodded at this too and Sam added: "Mind you, me and Alex coming along when we did saved them a big headache over what to do with you. I expect they were glad to get you off their hands so cheaply."

"Pig!" Nicky kicked Sam lightly on the shin. She had brightened up a lot since his and Alex's arrival, and having something to eat. She was almost too cheerful – and had even tucked into the toast and some not very appetising sandwiches left over from a staff member's packed lunch.

"Now I know what it is like to be really, really hungry, I'll never be so fussy again," she had said by way of explanation when Alex looked at her in surprise as they all wolfed the food down in the fuggy station staff room.

True to his old form, Alex finished his share first and looked so disappointed to see Nicky was well into her last slice of toast, that the station staff took pity and provided him with a pack of extra toast for the journey.

"Good of them to provide this too," he said as he dug the new pack out of his bag. "No one else wants any do they?" he asked hopefully, and was relieved when they shook their heads. "Great! I can eat the lot then. God I'm still so hungry I could eat the cling film too." He took a large mouthful.

"Pig!" Nicky repeated, this time addressing her brother.

"Some things never change!" Sam agreed, rolling his eyes. Alex just grinned, and continued chewing. But he nearly choked when he heard Sam's next comment.

Knowing how sensitive his sister was, he simply wouldn't have dared – not yet, not here, anyway. Besides, he thought, his sister would face plenty of questions from Mum and Dad when they got home. Much wiser to leave it to them, and just enjoy for now the quiet companionship of the three of them together. He'd done what he set out to do: he'd found his sister; they were all heading back home, tired and relieved; Nicky seemed happy; why spoil it? He could have kicked Sam - and not just a friendly joking tap either.

"So, Nicky, why did you set off in the middle of the night? Were you trying to track down your real mum?" Sam leant towards Nicky. Alex held his breath.

All Nicky's new-found cheerfulness seemed to evaporate in an instant. She sat back in her seat looking crushed and very small. Sam put his hand to his mouth.

"Oh damn. Nicky, I didn't mean to upset you, I'm sorry, I..."

"It's OK," Nicky said in a small voice. There was a long silence. "It's my fault – I thought Alex's mum – our mum – couldn't possibly care for me in the same way as she did for Alex, and I wanted to meet my real mum. Just see her, not even speak to her, just look and see if she looked and spoke like me, see where I belonged. Alex said I should wait, and I would have – honestly Alex – but there was something on the regional news about a murder in Birmingham, and as soon as the name 'Hitchin' was said, Mum switched off the telly and pretended the news was over and it was time for homework, whatever.

"So when I went upstairs I googled the news instead of starting my maths, and I knew then I was too late. I'd never meet my real mother now – but I had to go to the place where I thought she – my real mum, that is – had lived. I knew Mum and Dad wouldn't let me if I asked them – or you for that matter. So I just went," she ended lamely.

"And did you find the right place?" Alex was leaning forward now. Nicky nodded.

"Oh, Alex it was awful. I ..." She started to cry before she could finish her sentence.

"We know," said Alex. "And that creepy neighbour; did you see him too?"

Nicky nodded again. "He frightened me so I ran away, back to the main road, but I was so tired by that time, and I had cramp in both my legs. I thought I'd wait for a bus, but I was waiting for ages and I must have fallen asleep – and then that huge smelly tramp stole my bag and stuff, so I hid in the park for a bit. Then I ran all the way to the station – but I got lost and it took me ages. Then they wouldn't let me onto the platform because I didn't have a ticket. I cried, but that didn't help so I found a corner to hide.

"I don't know how long I'd been there but suddenly all those people kept coming up and asking questions and I didn't know what to do. I couldn't say anything, and I thought I'd never be able to speak again. Then they called the police because they thought I had run away from home. I hadn't, honestly, but I was too scared to say anything in case I got into more trouble. And then you came..." All her words came out in a great long gabble.

Alex patted her arm. "Seems you don't have a problem talking now!" he commented.

"But I'm fine with you and Sam – I was even dreaming about both of you, when that man stole my stuff. I dreamt you were coming to rescue me – and you did! Except I was on a beach in my dream, not in a smelly bus shelter." She paused, and then added with a wail: "But Alex, what am I going to say to Mum and Dad? They'll kill me!"

"Course not! They'll be more worried about why you felt the need to rush off and what the experience has done to you – you know Mum! But even I'm interested in how you feel about it all."

"Me too." It was the first time Sam had spoken for some time. His own feelings about what had happened to him recently were so confused he just felt numb. Did Nicky feel the same, he wondered.

Nicky thought for a while. "I don't feel anything at the moment. Well, I feel a bit stupid for rushing off, to be honest. That place - it didn't feel like home. I didn't feel part of that place at all. I'm just glad now we're going home – whatever Mum and Dad say when we get there."

"Just as well," said Alex. "Look we're just drawing into the station and – look! There are our parents. All four of them together."

"What? Not my mum and dad too?" Sam stared out of the window in astonishment.

The three of them jumped from their seats and rushed to the door of the carriage. They were the first off, and not since they were very little had they been so pleased to see their parents.

Mr. Rainsworth, normally so reserved and pre-occupied, almost ran towards his son and pulled him into a bear hug. Sam hugged him back then, peering out from under his dad's armpit to find his mother, he saw another train draw up and scores of people jump off and rush across the platform to catch the train the three of them had just left. Too late; with a squeal from the wheels as the brakes were released, the Birmingham-bound train gathered speed and left the station, leaving the passengers angry and disorientated at missing their connection. 'Just like we've all been these past few months,' he thought suddenly. He shook his head, startled by such a way of thinking, and reached out to squeeze his mum's hand. She squeezed it back but didn't say anything. She was, he noticed, almost smiling and he smiled back. He was relieved that she seemed neither angry nor upset. That was enough for now. There would be plenty of time for questions and explanations later.

Meanwhile, Nicky had rushed into her mum's open arms. "Mum I'm so sorry," she sobbed as Mrs. Stevens hugged her and stroked her hair. "I saw the news on the telly, and just had to go and see the place where Mum was killed." Mrs. Stevens took a step back. Still holding Nicky, she lifted her chin to look into her eyes.

"But my poor darling, that wasn't your mother." Mrs. Stevens sounded bewildered. "Why didn't you say that was what was bothering you?"

It was Nicky's turn to look bewildered. "But why did you switch the telly off? Why didn't you say it wasn't my mum? Who was it then?" Her look of bewilderment turned quickly to one of fury, and she pushed her mother away. Mrs. Stevens stepped back quickly, her hand to her mouth.

"Oh my God, what's happening Nicky, what have I done wrong now?"

Alex and his dad glanced at each other in alarm. It looked as though there was about to be another mother – daughter row. But this time, not in the privacy of their own home; not even just in front of close friends - which would be embarrassing enough; but right out there in public, in full view of every passer-by. Both father and son cringed.

Chapter Twenty-Nine

S am emerged from his dad's bear-like grip and looked at both his parents. They didn't look too startled by the set-to within the Stevens family – clearly all the parents had been talking to each other during the day. 'It might have helped,' he thought grimly, 'if they had talked to us a bit more recently – do they think we are still babies or something?'

He thought about his own situation, and how much easier it would have been to have it all out in the open from the start. If only they'd told him, he could have discussed it with Alex and come to terms with it much sooner. As Alex and Mrs. Rees had said – it wouldn't be the first time such a thing had happened, and it hadn't even come as much of a surprise to him really.

Mrs. Rees! The name jolted him into remembering his own situation and he clapped his hand to his mouth. "Oh shit!" he said, under his breath but just loud enough for his parents to hear. His dad didn't tell him off – rather it was as if he could read his mind.

"If you're worried about school and such, then stop – your mum and I have been in contact. Once we and the Stevens' had worked out that you were probably with Alex, and why, we let them and the police know. So you're not in any more trouble with either." When he'd finished speaking, his dad glanced over to the Stevens family. He nodded to his friend as he stood with Alex, a tense look on his face, then he turned back to his own wife and son.

"Come on, time to drop you both back home." He led them off to where his car was waiting. Sam jumped in the back and was pleased to notice his mum get into the front passenger seat with only the slightest hesitation. He just had time whilst on the drive back home to text Alex. *Hope u get sorted soon. cu 2mrw*

***

Alex read the text with a grim smile, as he sat in the back of his own dad's car, next to a silently weeping Nicky. His mum, also crying, sat next to his dad. His dad's face betrayed nothing of what he was feeling, but Alex noticed how tightly he was gripping the steering wheel – so tight his knuckles had gone white. He was glad when they reached their house and they could be released to go their separate ways.

But Mr. Stevens had a different idea. Normally he was the quiet placid parent, who happily left all the important decisions to his wife. But tonight he was the one in control.

"Come on, all of you – into the kitchen for a mug of tea. Nicky needs to know everything we know about her mother before we can move forward. I don't want this family to fall apart on my watch."

He turned to his daughter. "It isn't much, honestly my dear. What we kept from you we did for the best – what we thought was for the best, anyway. We really don't know much more than what was in that box Alex got out for you. But what we do know we're going to tell you now, once we've each got a drink in our hand."

Firmly, he ushered all his family into the kitchen, and supervised the making of tea and the retrieval of the biscuit tin from under a pile of clean laundry.

Then he started to talk.

Chapter Thirty

What are you doing tonight?"

The school bell had rung to mark the end of the day's lessons and Alex and Sam were packing their bags. Neither was in much hurry – most of the others had already left the classroom in one swift, noisy wave of pent-up energy that had been barely kept in check up to this point. The others were soon gone and the two boys looked at each other, enjoying the relative peace as the shouting, laughing horde moved further down the corridor.

"Dunno. Catch-up work from yesterday, I suppose."

Sam snorted. "Can't see why you'd bother with that. You probably know more about what you missed than the teachers giving the lessons. Now me, mind...."

"Quite so," Alex nodded in agreement. "That's why I need to get the work done – so as you can copy it and catch up."

Sam grinned. "Whatever! Perhaps we could do it together – then I could copy as you do it. Save time that way."

"OK." Alex nodded again. "Sounds fair enough. You provide some grub and I'll provide some brain. Unless, that is...." He stopped. He certainly didn't want his friend shoplifting again. Sam could see what he was thinking and interrupted quickly.

"No! It's sorted. There's plenty of food at home in the fridge – I checked this morning before I came out. Mum will be out, at least for a bit. So we'll have the place to ourselves."

"She's not ...." Alex thought of the last time he had been inside Sam's house and the sight of Mrs. Rainsworth drunk on the sofa. Again Sam could read his friend's mind.

"No fear of that happening again. At least I'm pretty sure of it. No, she's out with your mum – coffee in the cafeteria at the library, or something."

Alex nodded for the third time.

"Typical Mum - reading therapy! Sounds good to me – grub at your place, I mean, not the other."

Both boys had packed their bags by this time, and were hoisting them onto their shoulders.

"Perhaps it won't be a bad thing if our mums talk more. Maybe if they had done a bit more of that you and Nicky wouldn't have had to see a counsellor – yes she was due to meet Mrs Rees today too. I wonder how she got on."

"Mrs Rees? She's not so bad. Anyway I was just being a bit of an arsehole. It's Nicky I'm sorry for. How was she after last night?"

Alex paused before he spoke. "You know, I've never seen her so angry and upset – not even recently, and that's saying something. I don't know where she found the energy – she looked knackered after her adventures in Birmingham. But she just went on and on at Mum, and Dad a bit too. Dad wouldn't let any of us out of the kitchen; said we had to talk it out, which is a new one from him – he hates rows. Anyway, after a bit, he said Nicky should shut up and listen to Mum as she needed to tell her something." Alex paused again, his eyes closed and he shivered slightly as if re-living the unpleasantness of the night before.

"And?" Sam prompted him after a while.

"And, basically, after saying how sorry she was to upset Nicky, Mum said that if she had thought it through properly she would have told her that the news report of the woman killed was about one of her real mum's relatives – her sister or something. Mum knew from Social Services that Nicky's mum had left to make a new life in Australia with a new boyfriend to get away from the whole Hitchin gang as they were all criminals or prostitutes. She'd switched the telly off quickly because she wasn't ready to answer any questions from Nicky, and hadn't realised Nicky had heard the all-important name – and certainly not thought about what Nicky might do about that information."

"Wow, so what happens next? It's not all peace and quiet in your place now surely?"

"Early days! Signs are good so far though. Mum is liaising with Social Services about Nicky finding out a bit more about her real mum – she left details with them apparently so Nicky could contact her if she wanted to when she was old enough."

"Cool! Pity she hadn't spoken to your sister earlier, but that's parents for you – they think they're protecting their kids from some unbearable truth, whereas in fact it's unbearable to them. It's the not knowing that hurts us." Alex realised that Sam was thinking of his own parents as well as the situation with Nicky, and touched his arm.

"You're dead right there."

Both boys fell silent, Alex marvelling a bit about the new, more thoughtful, reflective side his friend seemed to be developing – he wasn't just going to be a sports fiend with the looks that would soon make him the centre of female attention.

Sam, meanwhile, was remembering that he should have brought his kit for rugby practice. 'Damn,' he thought, 'I'll have lost my place in the team for the next game.' Still he could always get back up to speed next week – his meetings with the police and the youth offending team should be out of the way by then and, with a bit of effort, he'd soon regain his place.

He was also thinking about Nicky, and how pretty she had looked yesterday, despite the grimy face, the tears and the air of utter dejection about her when they found her at the station. Alex was a lucky devil having a sister like that.

Alex broke out of his reverie first. He looked down the school drive and gave a slight start.

"Hey, if we want to get the bus home, we'd better

get a move on." He broke into a run.

Sam tugged at his sleeve, to hold him back.

"I'd rather walk – and look, here's your sister coming down the drive, she's going to miss it as well."

"Oh yes, she was seeing Mrs. Rees. OK if she walks with us?"

"That's fine." Sam looked back up the drive and watched as Nicky came towards them. Her eyes lit up when she saw her brother – gangly, spotty, awkward, clever Alex. And Sam felt a slight stab of disappointment that they had not lit up for him. Refreshed after a night in her own bed, with her hair washed and gleaming, she really was one of the best looking girls in the school. Alex was a lucky sod to have such a sister.

Nicky smiled at Sam shyly as she came alongside the two boys.

"Hallo."

"Hallo," he said back. There was a slight pause.

"Thanks for coming to rescue me with Alex yesterday."

"It was nothing – I just came to keep Alex out of trouble really." Sam could have kicked himself for such a dumb answer, but Nicky was shaking her head vigorously.

"No, it was more than that – you see, it was..." she paused as she struggled, and failed, to find the right words. Instead she took his hand and squeezed it briefly.

Sam found himself blushing, and it didn't help that Alex chose that moment to nudge him quite painfully in the ribs and pinch his arm.

"Ow – gerroff!" He turned on his friend reproachfully, but Alex was by then looking the other way and picking at a new crop of spots with an air of innocence. Sam turned back to Nicky.

"Alex is coming back to my place for tea – I'm cooking. Do you want to come too?"

Her eyes lit up. This time he was sure it was for

him.

"Oh yes please! But Alex, please stop scratching – you know Mum says it just makes things worse."

"Yes Miss!" Alex reluctantly tore his hand away from his face and they walked on for a few minutes in companionable silence before Nicky spoke again.

"You two – you're great you know. The way you worked out where I was and came and found me. You should set up a detective agency."

"It was a complete fluke," said Alex dismissively, just as Sam was replying:

"Good idea, but you would have to be part of it – after all, you found that address first!"

"But what else is there to detect?" Alex sounded genuinely puzzled.

"Well you could find out who was sending me those horrid texts about being so fat for starters."

Sam looked at her in surprise.

"But you're not fat. You must be the best looking girl in your class." He nudged his friend before adding: "Certainly the best looker in the Stevens family."

"Oh well, we'll think about it." Alex cut in quickly, not liking the way the conversation seemed to be going. "But first things first, what did you say about food and your place? I'm ..."

"Starving!" All three chorused together.

Linking arms, they left the school grounds and set off down the road for the long walk home as the late November sun glimpsed fitfully around the gathering clouds. They stopped for a moment to look up as the sun finally sank beneath the horizon leaving, briefly, a pink and gold tinge to the cloudscape. Now they would have to walk most of the way in the dark; but tomorrow was going to be OK.

The End

About the Author:

I have lived in The United Kingdom all my life. I have worked with the Probation Service, the Police Authority, as a Charity boss, and as a freelance child protection consultant. I currently sit on the boards of two charities: one that runs assessment centres for families experiencing problems, and one that provides services for the elderly (well, you've got to think ahead...)

I enjoy reading and the theatre. I try to keep fit by swimming and racing my cairn terrier round the park. He usually wins.

Acknowledgements:

My husband, Rick, and son, Rob, April Chaplin, Ann Evans, and others in the Coventry Writers' group. Special thanks must go to the staff at Solstice Publishing for all their guidance and support.

Social media:

Facebook: https://www.facebook.com/pages/Margaret-Egrot/1374506486178952

Twitter: https://twitter.com/meegrot

Made in the USA
Charleston, SC
11 January 2015